Pack

His Luna

Ktty

Imagination Inspires Reality—Janesville, WI
Paperback ISBN: 979-8-218-43378-9
eBook ISBN: 979-8-3302-8681-2
Title: *Pack: His Luna*
Author: Ktty
Digital distribution | 2024
Paperback | 2024

Published in the United States by New Book Authors Publishing

Dedication

This story is for many people. For starters, myself. Publishing has always been a dream of mine and now I am accomplishing that. Let this story be proof to any and everyone. No dream is too small or childish. If there's something you've wanted to do, let me be the push you need. Do it.

For my best friend who inspired this story. Let your imagination run wild. Your talent and creativity are wasted behind that desk.

For all my family members who saw this coming since I first brought it up at four years old. Get your told you so's out now, I know it's coming. Also... Sorry for the genre. I can hear the phone calls coming in already about my descriptive nature and choice of words in certain scenes.

For my mother-in-law. Thank you for your constant and unwavering support. If it wasn't for the small acts of kindness through this process, I don't think I would've had the drive to make this a reality.

To the Twitch streamer Simsav. If not for your kindness and the support of the community you've created, I would've never had the energy to write this to begin with or continue when I started to lose steam. You guys truly never miss a beat. Babs, I know this isn't the dark books we crave but I promise I'll work on one just for you down the road.

To the D&D groups I've played with. Thank you for not judging me for the work I've done in the middle of our sessions. As awkward as it was to write some of this while you guys were around. Aimed at me or not, the laughs were much appreciated. I look forward to your input on the future of this story.

Lastly. My son and my fiancé. Thank you both for being the light guiding me through this. Nicholas, your love has inspired many hearts in the characters I've written. Your determination in everything you do is incredibly infectious and I adore you more than you know for that alone. Kurt, allow this accomplishment of mine to be proof that no matter the road you choose when the time comes, Mommy will always support it no matter how small or vast.

To the readers who've decided to give my words a chance. I hope to see you all throughout this journey and the jungle juice that is truly my brain spilled out into every page.

I could go on for pages about the support I've received, but I won't hold you up any further. Go on and enjoy, Little one. Greyson is waiting.

Chapter One

Following an unfamiliar path was never something I thought I'd ever do. I've never been the kind of girl to stray from what I knew was safe but given the events of the past week… It was time I took a risk. The path I followed led up a mountain, nowhere near as large scale as Mt. Everest, but just as difficult to traverse. It was dark, and I knew the danger of the forest at night, but for some reason, I felt safer, and the forest felt more vibrant, more alive. I stood on the path, admiring the flora and fauna I passed, that was, until… I smelled something. It was familiar, comforting, warm, and cold at the same time. I abandoned the trail hesitantly at first, but the longer I followed the scent the more intoxicating it became. My senses overwhelmed and my mind was rendered useless, I didn't stop until my legs gave out from exhaustion.

Collapsing to the dirt beneath me snapped me from my euphoric trance and I realized I had gotten myself completely lost…

"Great going Naph," I muttered in frustration to myself.

I rubbed my sore and throbbing legs, hoping to return to my feet soon. I sat on the damp ground paying little to no attention to my surroundings, my judgement still clouded from a false sense of safety.

A twig in the near distance snapping caught my attention, and I begrudgingly got to my feet, with the help of leaning against a tree now realizing just how defenseless I truly was. There was nothing in my immediate vicinity to use to defend myself so instead I did my best to mask my fear. I brushed a stray lock of hair behind my ear and listened more intently, trying my damndest to use abilities I had yet to figure out. Another twig snapped, and the sound was getting closer. My breath caught in my throat and I shook the nerves off.

"Who's there?!" I shouted, praying for an innocent animal that wouldn't cause me any harm. I felt my confidence wavering as the sound kept growing closer, the pace not slowing. I was in trouble and I knew it.

"My, how far you've strayed," a voice boomed from the shadows. "Who are you, and what are you doing in my territory?" The voice echoed through the trees. I felt a sense of fear pang at my heart as well as a calm washing over me. The feelings fought, conflicting with my reaction.

"What's it to you?" I scoffed stupidly. I knew my reaction would either make or break me. What was I doing?

The source of the voice chuckled, it was a sweet symphony that reeled me in and made my hair stand on end simultaneously. "Don't test my patience little one. State your business," the voice demanded. My knees felt weak and my brain was compelled to command.

"I got lost," I admitted.

"Lost? Am I to believe that to be the truth?" The voice huffed.

All sense of safety snapped. I was left with a subtle tremor, stuck in place like petrified stone. A man strode out from the shadows, standing at least one foot taller than my small 5'. He was well-groomed and his eyes flashed with an overwhelming amount of pride and danger.

"It... It is the truth..." I stuttered out, I felt an urge to defend myself but knew it was useless against a man with a muscular build like the man who stood before me.

He could probably snap me like the twigs beneath our feet with ease and not waste a breath. A low guttural growl came from him, followed by a wicked grin. "If that's the truth, then how did you stray from the path little one?"

A small but alluring chuckle escaped him. I began to feel like prey, and he was my predator.

"I was following the path, I got distracted," I explained without giving too much.

He regarded me with a contemplative eye, his gaze making me feel as though my soul was bare before him. "Distracted?" His eyes narrowed, making my already small size feel that much smaller.

"Y-yes," I stuttered.

My breathing became labored as that smell returned. My eyes darted around, it was close, I could feel it, it was calling me. I could feel my senses being clouded once more and all of my reasoning left me. The world around me began to fade and all that mattered was finding the source of the scent I craved more than my safety. Intoxicating wasn't enough to describe the scent that lingered in the air.

"What distracted you little one?" his voice echoed in my head.

Compelled to answer with no sense of reasoning left, I uttered, "Home."

My eyes were heavy, half-lidded, I felt my body swaying with the breeze that carried the sweet scent of belonging. His tempting laughter wasn't enough to snap me from the trance I was in.

"What's your name little one?" He raised an eyebrow as he spoke, he seemed unconvinced of my honesty.

Still entranced. "Naphinae, Naphinae Kent." My name rolled off my tongue without hesitation. It was unsettling how easily my words left my lips, it made my skin crawl.

I watched as the man approached me, his expression unchanged and unreadable. I couldn't break from my trance to move away. I was frozen in place. His hands found their way to my shoulders.

"Little one? Are you alright?" His expression softened, a hint of concern hidden behind the beautiful broken blue hue of his eyes. The sweet scent the air carried got stronger and the moment his hands left my shoulders, moving down to the bare skin of my arms was like my skin ignited completely engulfed in flames, like a fever I'd never experienced.

My trance-like state broke as I doubled over holding myself groaning and biting my lip to avoid the release of screams my body craved. The heat building up within me was unbearable. The man knelt in front of me, concern written across his face. Tears stung my eyes, threatening to fall. I couldn't bear the pain and a pained, strained scream escaped me as I fell to my knees leaving me breathless. Before I knew it, the man picked me up carrying me bridal style, his arms enveloping me with strength and ease. I clung to him as if my life depended on it.

I had no idea where he was taking me and I didn't care, it was better than lying on the dirt.

"Stay with me little one."

He held me tighter and his words rattled in my head as the burning sensation intensified. I held on to him tighter as a gush of wind rushed past us and he stopped dead in his tracks.

"There's no way," he muttered, I felt his entire demeanor shift. He started to move again, and his hold on me became more protective.

We got to a house and it was all a blur, my pain becoming increasingly harder to fight off.

"Just hang on Naphinae." His voice sounded more worried. He carried me into a room and laid me down on a bed, although comfort wasn't something I could feel through the amount of pain I was in. "We need to get you out of these clothes." He tried to sound calm but his tone was laced with urgency.

A low groan escaped my lips, every breath becoming a battle. My skin felt as if I was nothing but flame, all of my senses rendered me defenseless.

"I'm going to get you out of these clothes now, okay? But I need you to do your best to hold still and not move too much, can you do that?" His tone was soft hinting toward compassion.

My body temperature rose to an unbearable level, a soft sob escaping me despite my best efforts. I bit my lip to keep from whimpering as he worked to remove my clothes. His touch was gentle but commanding, every graze setting a new fire to ignite in my skin.

"I know it's difficult, but you're doing great." He did his best to sound gentle and concerned but there was an underlying sense of urgency that made my anxiety heighten.

I gritted my teeth, my body beginning to shake with every breath as I felt consumed by the fire beneath my skin.

He began to instruct me, "I need you to focus on your breathing. Inhale deeply, exhale slowly."

Although soft, his voice was still commanding. My chest heaved with every breath, every inhale punctuated by a pain-filled groan on exhale.

"Just keep breathing Naphinae." His tone shifted, firm but calming.

"Make… it stop…" I panted, I resorted to begging. I couldn't take the pain anymore.

He responded with urgency, "I know it's hard, keep breathing, and focus on the sound of my voice." His voice was soothing, like a childhood lullaby.

My body shuttered with each ragged breath I took, my tears bringing temporary relief.

"Please... Make it stop…" I begged again, it felt like my cries were falling on deaf ears. I shut my eyes tightly, screaming out in agony.

"Listen to me, this is going to be difficult, but I need you to trust me. Can you do that?" The urgency in his tone faded to compassion.

I felt safe despite the burning sensation not wavering. I nodded hesitantly, tears still streaming down my face.

Although his tone was serious, it wasn't as commanding, "I need you to focus on my voice. Nothing else matters right now. Can you do that for me?"

The sound of his gentle tone sent a shiver up my spine and shot butterflies straight into my stomach. I nodded, any movement agitating the fire that was set ablaze within me.

I was desperate for relief. I didn't care about the consequences. I could hear the sound of his belt unbuckling and the subtle rustling of his clothes being removed.

"Naphinae, I need you to listen carefully." His voice was tender yet commanding causing my ragged breathing to catch in my throat. I opened my eyes, a strange mixture of trust and pain driving my courage as my eyes wandered across his toned and muscular body. He approached me slowly. "You need to stay perfectly still. This is going to hurt, but it will only last for a moment. Do you understand?"

He spoke gently but his words were firm, eliciting a sense of calm over my quaking body. I was filled with fear and anticipation. I bit my lip to suppress my urge to scream out again.

He positioned himself on top of me, his blue eyes reflecting compassion and care. "I promise it'll be over soon. Hold on to me if you need to."

His words were sincere and soothing. I nodded, every breath I took hitching on inhale. His expression became serious.

"Stay calm and focus on me. I'm going to make this quick, okay?" he spoke gently, his tone betraying his exterior demeanor. Tears streamed down my face, my pain overwhelming. "Shh, I know it's hard. I got you."

The attempt he made to comfort me despite the gravity of the situation didn't go unnoticed. I felt him push into me and my immediate reaction was to cling to him. I gripped his shoulders for support, digging my nails into his skin, as he met with the resistance of my innocence, my virginity. My tears fell faster, silently begging for all of my pain to wash away.

"Just breathe Naphinae, I've got you." He gently caressed my hair as his voice came out strained but firm.

I buried my face into his neck trying my damndest to block out the pain. He grunted softly in my ear sending another shiver up my spine, clearly feeling the tension but he maintained control making me his primary focus. "I know, just hold on. Keep breathing." His voice was laced with concern but overridden by pain as my nails dug further into his shoulders.

My cries echoed in the room, mingling with his groans of pleasure and pain. The sensations were more than I thought I could handle. He wrapped his arm around me, drawing me closer, trying to offer me comfort amidst the turmoil I was facing.

"I'm sorry, I know it hurts. This will pass, I promise." The reassurance in his voice calmed me.

His hand cradled my face, gently caressing my cheekbone with his thumb, wiping away the tears that escaped me. With each thrust my body trembled with the pain, my tears never ceasing. He held my head to his chest gently stroking my hair as he kept his movements slow and rhythmic. "Just breathe, you'll get through this."

His words were calming although his breathing told another story, a story of compassion and pleasure. The pain, the pleasure, the cries… all melded into a symphony of sensations, all new, all overwhelming. Continuing his best attempts to comfort me his words were authoritative, commanding, but gentle, "You're doing great Naphinae. Just focus on my voice."

As he sunk further into me, my body betrayed my mask, my cries becoming more for passion than pain. Although the pain was still more than evident, it paved the way to pleasure that was building within me. A complete stranger holding such power over me.

Going against my better judgment to keep my eyes closed, I opened them and looked up at the stranger. His blue eyes were darkened by desire, by lust, it drove him along with his concern for my well-being. He gritted his teeth as he continued grinding his hips against mine.

"Stay with me Naphinae." His voice was strained yet calm, his rough exterior faltering.

My body continued to tremble in his embrace as his hips rocked into mine, my grip on his shoulders tightened breaking his skin as my nails dug in further. My cries of pain now of pleasure blending in perfect harmony with his grunts and groans. Each thrust ignited a new flame no longer of pain but a drive to keep the pleasure we were both feeling to keep going. He hugged me closer, leaning down to whisper in my ear, "You're doing so well Naphinae."

His voice was no longer soothing but full of praise, his hunger became insatiable. A primal force filling both of us.

Before I could process what was happening, his teeth sunk into my shoulder clamping down like a bear trap. I screamed out in agony, my voice echoing off the walls, I didn't dare to pull away. He held me tighter. His body began trembling, his emotions conflicting and more than evident in his body's response. He was enjoying this but his main focus was still to help me through what I was experiencing. I felt fear and confusion, his teeth sinking further into my shoulder and breaking through my skin. His need began to surface, a hunger igniting in his eyes. I did my best to endure everything that was happening, I gritted my teeth and anchored myself in the moment. His hunger began to consume him the way the pain was consuming me, he fought against his primal instinct to continue to bring comfort to me as his teeth continued to sink further into my shoulder.

I tangled my fingers in his hair, I felt trust in this moment despite my pain. My movement sent him into overdrive as he began to move against me losing his rhythm, his hunger sending him into a fit rocking his hips into me with reckless abandon. I surrendered to the moment, my hands gripping at his hair as much as I fought against it. My better nature was gone replaced by something animalistic. My back arched, pressing my body against him, a soft gasp escaping me. I held him closer as his movements became more erratic and his teeth sunk even further into my shoulder, the intensity of the moment and the connection we shared intensifying in ways indescribable. All restraint he had was broken.

He released my now-bleeding shoulder and kissed me with such a hunger that it felt like he wanted to devour me. The kiss was unexpected but welcomed, I responded in kind meeting his passion every bit as eager and unrestrained. His hands began to explore my body, every curve, every inch, his touch becoming more aggressive as his loss of control became more obvious. I gripped his hair and pulled him closer, my ferocity matching his. His mouth moved back down to my shoulder, breaking the kiss. I whimpered, my lips tingling at the loss of his. Every breath I took invited him, my mind blank except for him and this moment. I gripped his hair tighter urging him on. His hands continued to explore as he kissed my shoulder lovingly, his touch aggressive and hungry, his every movement consumed by pure animalistic desire. My back arched pressing against him again, every nerve in my body tingling with anticipation. I surrendered completely, giving myself over to the moment entirely, my mind body, and soul enthralled with every fiber of my being.

His lips returned crashing against mine, devastatingly hungry. I pulled him as close as I could, our desires aligning, intertwining. I relished in every passing moment, my hands beginning to trace the contours of his back. His touch became more forceful, gripping my hips tightly with increased urgency. His desire was fueled by my own. My body began to tighten around him, an unfamiliar knot twisting in my stomach. My nails dug into his back, breaking through his skin effortlessly and without hesitation. My cries of pleasure were replaced by whimpers as the unfamiliar feeling took hold of me. His control slipped completely, and his grip on my hips tightened as he drove into me with a speed and power I didn't know possible.

A primal response I didn't know I was capable of taking me without warning, I dragged my nail down his back as I bit down on his shoulder hard enough to draw blood causing me to unravel. His hold on me became even more possessive with each passing second, a low growl coming from him as I bit down even harder. The sound of our pleasure echoed throughout the room, an intimate harmony of our hips rocking against one another and our cries of pleasure.

With one final surge of pure passion and pure desire, our screams echoed out in unison, a moment of pure ecstasy as we unraveled. We both collapsed against the bed, completely spent but completely satisfied. The overwhelming heat I had felt was now gone, replaced by exhaustion and contentment.

Chapter Two

As we lay there both attempting to catch our breath, his hand came up to my face capturing my attention as he began to caress my cheek, still struggling to catch his breath. I leaned into his touch, my eyes softening as I struggled to catch my breath myself. He continued to caress my face, his touch becoming more gentle and losing its possessive nature. I stared into his broken blue eyes, his emotions reflecting my own. I placed my hand gently over his, a small smile on my face. He brushed a strand of hair from my face as his gaze softened further. Unsure of what came over me, I giggled. He smiled back as he brushed the stray strand of hair behind my ear. With a sudden urge of courage, I broke the silence.

"I realize you were so caught up interrogating me, I never caught your name handsome." I giggled again.

With a shy smile, he spoke, "I'm Greyson, Greyson Carver. But everyone calls me Grey."

I felt a blush creeping into my cheeks as my smile widened. With a nervous laugh that caught me off guard, he continued, "It's nice to meet you properly Naphinae."

He looked into my eyes deeply. I held his gaze, feeling nothing but admiration as my hand found its way to rest against his chest.

"I could get lost in those beautiful eyes of yours." His voice was as gentle as his touch. I could feel a rush as the connection between us grew stronger. I felt my heart skip a beat and suddenly my mask fell leaving me feeling vulnerable and shy as if my soul was out for him to see. His smile became softer as he leaned in to whisper, "You're a rare gem, Naphinae Kent."

His touch became even more gentle, something I would've never known he was capable of based on our initial encounter. I felt my heart flutter in my chest, melting into his touch. His gaze locked with mine, his touch becoming increasingly possessive. "I've never met anyone quite like you before Naphinae." His voice was soft and gentle, caressing my heart with his words. The intensity of the moment was beyond palpable.

He leaned in, his voice becoming even softer as he whispered, "I want to hold you in my arms every night, and wake up to see your face every morning."

His touch was intoxicating and possessive as he gripped me tightly, pulling me in for a passionate kiss. The kiss deepened as the world around us disappeared. I broke the kiss, leaning my forehead against his. He looked into my eyes, a smile playing on his lips.

I sat up, my body sore, but I managed nonetheless.

"Let me help you." He chuckled. He helped me, pulling me up into a sitting position.

"So you're the alpha of this pack?" I questioned. I was both in awe and intrigued. He nodded in response as he leaned in kissing my neck. I giggled at the sensation, "Hey! That tickles!"

He chuckled as he pulled away with a mischievous grin.

I had so many questions but had no idea how to ask any of them. The way he looked at me with hunger and with such an intensity of caring made me want to melt and never leave his bed. Almost as if he could read my mind. "Go ahead, ask me anything you want." He smiled softly, his tone gentle and understanding.

I looked into his eyes. I admired him and I don't know why. He gave me a kind smile as he waited patiently for me to start asking my questions. I returned his smile. "Where do I start?"

He grinned. "You can start with anything you want. Take your time Naphinae."

He gently tucked a strand of hair behind my ear, resting his hand on my chin so I would look at him as I asked my questions.

I hesitated but asked my first question despite my fear. "How did you know how to help me?" I furrowed my eyebrows as I spoke, genuinely interested as to what just happened to me.

His smile softened as his hand moved from my chin to the side of my face gently caressing my cheekbone with his thumb.

"I knew the signs," he spoke with a hint of concern as his eyes roamed over the features that made my face.

"The signs? The signs of what?" My curiosity peaked getting the better of me.

He leaned in close before he spoke. "Signs of someone going into heat." His voice was soft and gentle, lulling me into a sense of safety. My eyes narrowed in confusion as he spoke.

"Heat?"

He nodded. "Yes, heat. It's a natural process, it happens to some females when they reach a certain age." His tone remained soft and caring.

I felt even more confused, I swear my eyebrows were practically knit together at this point. "But I'm 22 and never experienced that before, why now?"

He chuckled softly and tightened his grip on me, his forehead now resting against mine. "It could be a delayed reaction to stress or another trigger."

At this point, I felt I had more questions than answers.

"What other trigger could there be Greyson?" I felt a pang of anxiety smack me like a ton of bricks.

He looked into my eyes before speaking again, it was almost like he found this amusing. "It could be triggered by certain things, like scents or sounds."

I remember the smell that made me stray from the trail and that didn't make me feel any better. I had no idea what that meant, I broke eye contact and looked down. "So, scent in my case? That smell that distracted me from the trail?" I waited for him to answer. He nodded again, his hold on me tightened as he nuzzled into my hair.

"Yes, that's a common trigger." His voice was laced with concern.

I shook off the concern in his voice. "But that makes no sense Greyson... I didn't start burning up until you touched me."

He grinned at my words, a sense of pride in his eyes. "Naphinae, that's because your body knew what it wanted. It knew it was safe with me." His gaze fixated on mine as I looked back up at him.

I shook my head. I felt my frustration growing. "I feel like you're leaving something out, what aren't you telling me?"

He pulled me closer, his grip tight and possessive once more.

"I can't tell you everything Naphinae." He looked into my eyes as he spoke and although his tone was soft and kind my blood boiled.

I moved away from him and looked him in the eye as a low growl came from my throat, shocking myself at the reaction I had but not letting it show. "What aren't you telling me?"

He leaned in closer to me and growled in return like he was challenging me. His eyes narrowed. The look in his eyes sent a shiver down my spine. "I've already told you more than I should have."

I felt my frustration reach its boiling point, any filter I had now gone. "Oh? Do tell, what is the big bad alpha wolf so scared to say that I can't know the truth behind what triggered my heat?"

I knew once the words left my lips it was a mistake, but one I couldn't take back. His growl became even more intense, he stared at me with a mixture of anger and concern.

"You have no idea what you're getting yourself into little one."

I decided to play him at his own game, he wanted a power struggle… I'd give him one. "Try me."

My gaze challenged his. Inside I was petrified but I didn't let it rattle me, I needed to know what he was hiding. His growl reached a crescendo as he lunged at me, pinning me down against the bed with a force that seemed to surprise him. I yelped as he pinned me, my wrists immediately feeling like putty beneath his grip. I persisted nonetheless, "What are you hiding Greyson? What triggered my heat?!"

His growl softened but his grip on my wrists didn't. He leaned in closer, his voice barely a whisper, "I'll tell you, but first, you need to understand something." His voice was stern and commanding.

I continued to challenge him. "What do I need to understand?" I huffed.

He bit my neck gently before pulling away and looking me in the eyes, a soft growl escaped his lips before he spoke. "You are mine. I will keep you safe, and I will take care of you. But I cannot allow anyone else to have you." His growling ceased, and he spoke with a hint of sadness in his tone.

It surprised me and it pained me to see him that way but again, I didn't let it show. "What aren't you telling me?"

He leaned in closer. "You're my mate Naphinae." His grip tightened as he pulled me closer to him.

I was in disbelief, not only did I find my mate but he was the alpha of his pack? I was more than sure that my disbelief was written across my face. "So I was in heat because I met you? My mate?"

His grip was enough to make me yelp as it tightened further. The look in his eyes reflected longing and possessiveness. "Yes, Naphinae."

I tried to get out of his grip. "Y-you're hurting me…"

He immediately released his grip and looked down at me with concern in his eyes.

"I'm sorry Naphinae." His words seemed genuine.

I brought my wrists down and rubbed them to ease the tension. "How is it possible for me to go into heat and find you if I've never shifted?"

He helped me to sit up again, giving me a bit of space as he grabbed my wrists gently and massaged them for me.

"You must have a latent ability to shift little one."

"I'm not exactly sure what that means Greyson."

For some reason my words made him smile. I'm not sure if it was because he was able to share these moments with me or if my lack of knowledge gave him the power to tell me what he deemed fit.

"It means that you have the potential to shift, you just haven't discovered it yet."

I listened to his words and as they processed, "So I've been capable all this time?" The words left me before I could even think about what I wanted to say. Geez, curiosity really did kill the cat.

He nodded. "Yes," he said, simply.

Again my words slipped, "Can you teach me how?"

A hint of pride flashed in his eyes. He seemed almost excited by the idea. "Of course, I'll teach you everything you need to know."

I don't know what came over me but I felt frustrated by the entirety of this situation. "Let me guess, when you feel I'm ready."

He chuckled at my question. "You catch on quickly little one." His voice was gentle yet commanding.

My anger got the better of me and I growled at him defiantly.

"I suggest you watch your tone little one." His tone remained calm but his voice was drenched with danger.

"I have been hidden away for years! I'll be dammed if I let you tell me when I can shift when I wasn't even sure I could!" My growling became more guttural as my defiance shined through, a glow reflecting from me against him. Was it my eyes? What the hell was happening? His growl matched pitch with mine, his eyes glowing an amber.

"Naphinae, you do not understand the danger you're putting yourself in."

A dangerous growl escaped me, my anger reaching a peak. "I'm tired of being told what I can and can't do!" I felt my blood begin to boil.

"Then you leave me no choice." His voice grew deeper, his eyes blazing with a determination that any other moment would've made me back down. Not this time.

I stood to my feet defying him completely, a glow reflecting against him as my growling intensified. He stood to his feet as well, towering over me. He growled in response to my defiance, standing his ground. "You do NOT want to test me little one."

My growl became a snarl, baring my fangs at him, the glow reflecting against him glowing brighter. His growl overpowered mine, his eyes glowing with a stronger intensity than before as he moved forward pinning me against the wall. I snarled again, refusing to back down.

What an idiot…

His grip on me tightened as he leaned in closer, his growling wavering momentarily. "Naphinae, please. I don't want to hurt you. Just listen to me."

I snarled again and tried to push him off, fighting with everything I had in me.

His grip tightened further. "Naphinae, don't make me do this."

I glared at him with a pure rage I never knew I could possess, my snarl deepening as I stood my ground trying to push him off of me.

With one swift movement, I managed to free myself from his grip. His eyes flashed with a mixture of surprise and determination. "So be it."

I stood my ground challenging him. "I am not your puppet or your plaything Greyson."

His growl deepened to the point the entire room shook, his voice echoing off the walls as he stood to his full height and stared down at me with a rage that would shake me to my core. "I am the alpha wolf Naphinae."

Before I could challenge him and his authority further, a sharp pain that radiated through me brought me to my knees screaming in pain. He approached me cautiously, his growl fading quickly as he became concerned. "Little one! Are you okay?"

My body shook again but this time the pain was amplified beyond what I experienced with heat. He knelt before me, any traces of anger or authority gone and replaced by a calm and soothing nature. "It's okay. The pain will pass."

Another sharp pain radiated through me, ripples of pain worse than anything I could've ever imagined. The sound of my bones snapping bounced off the walls and echoed through my head on a loop, replaying my pain over and over. I screamed in pure agony as tears streamed down my face. "It…hurts…" I panted.

He placed a gentle hand on my shoulder. "I know little one, but you're doing it."

His voice washed a sense of relief over me. My shoulder snapped beneath his hand, and another agonizing scream escaped me. "I'm right here. I won't let anything hurt you." My bones one by one snapped and realigned, leaving me in a constant state of pure agony.

He stood close by me, attempting to comfort me through this but it fell on deaf ears as a ringing shot through my ears. "Focus on my voice. You can do this."

I did my best to focus on him, on anything. Every snap and shift in my bones' alignment sent a new ripple of pain through me, like an endless ocean and I was caught in the current.

This felt like a fate worse than death.

He brushed his hand through my hair, stroking my hair at a constant rhythm giving me something to focus on. "Just focus on me, let me ground you. Let the feeling anchor you, you're almost there I promise."

I sobbed, my tears falling almost as constantly as he stroked his fingers through my hair.

"It… feels like… I'm tearing… apart…." The pain was so intolerable I couldn't hear the sound of my voice.

"It's only a matter of time now. Keep anchoring to the feeling of me, you'll make it through this, I promise." His voice was calm and gentle, doing his best to console me, to comfort me.

"I… I can't… it… hurts…" Speaking became a battle. One I didn't have the strength to fight.

"You can, I know you can. Just a little longer, it'll be over soon."

I clung to the sound of his voice like a lifeline, as if my very being depended on it. My sobs interspersed with a sharp gasp as my face felt like it was being hit by a truck. My teeth felt like they were being pulled, and my skull felt like it shattered.

"You're so close." He attempted to encourage me but it felt like a battle lost.

A low growl came straight from my core, something purely inhuman. "I know it's painful, but keep holding on. Just a little longer, your shift is almost complete." He held me closer to him, stroking my hair remaining the only constant my mind would let me focus on. His touch was loving and patient, more than I was with him before my bones started breaking.

Note to self, quit being a bitch and people just may surprise you.

With a final scream, my body finished its first shift, the pain subsiding leaving nothing but a dull ache in its wake. He let go of a breath I'm sure he didn't know he was holding as I stood before him. He looked into my eyes.

"There she is." His voice was drenched with pride and admiration, his gaze was loving and supportive. So many emotions that remained unspoken but reflected in those broken yet beautiful blue eyes.

Chapter Three

I howled as a sense of accomplishment and overall relief washed over me, the ocean's relentless tidal waves leaving me to enjoy my new form.

"Well done little one," Greyson's voice shook with emotion as a smile graced his face.

So many new unfamiliar feelings hit me all at once. My tail thumped against the floor as I looked up at him. His fingers ruffled my fur.

"You should be proud of yourself little one." His voice was full of affection as he gazed upon my new form. I attempted to stand on all fours, I was a bit wobbly. He helped me to stand. "Take it slow, your body is still adjusting to the shift."

I adapted quickly to the new sensation and stood on my own. I walked around getting a feel for my movement. My paws pattered softly against the flooring beneath me.

I geared up and bolted toward him, tackling him to the ground as a low playful growl escaped me. He laughed and reciprocated my playful growl, playfully wrestling with me as he wrapped his arms around me. "Now, now, you've got to be careful with your new strength."

The smell of home, the same smell that brought me here, lingered in the air. I brought down my snout and sniffed him, the exact source of the intoxicating scent. Unbeknownst to me, my tail was wagging with excitement, something that will probably take years for me to get familiar with. He allowed me to sniff him and nuzzled against me in kind.

"Curious, aren't you?" He laughed.

Without hesitation, and I should've had some, I licked him before bouncing off him to explore a bit. He chuckled, his eyes following my every movement. "Go ahead and explore little one. Just be careful not to stray too far from me."

I turned back to him with my ears perked up and howled. He smiled at my response, his eyes shifting from me to the window and the full moon in the night sky surrounded by the stars. "I'm glad you made it through your first shift Naphinae. This is only the beginning." His tone was wistful, to say the least. What a sap.

I came across a mirror and hopped up on my hind legs, resting my front paws against the mirror to get a better look at myself. My fur was pure white, like the snow, but I had patches of ash blonde, and almost a faded grey throughout my fur. My eyes were a glowing golden color that rendered even me speechless.

He came up behind me and ran his hand through my fur. "You're beautiful little one. And your fur is so soft."

I enjoyed the affection and leaned into his touch, a low rumble coming from my chest and my tail thumping against the floor.

He chuckled and continued to pet me. "I'm glad you find this comforting."

I turned and sat in front of him, my tail still wagging.

He smiled and crouched down to my eye level. "So, little one…."

I tilted my head curiously wondering what he could want to say. He brought his hand up to scratch behind my ear. I prayed this moment would be a myth but sure enough, my foot thumped against the floor no matter how much I willed it to stop.

He laughed at my reaction but his smile remained once his laughter stopped. "What would you like to do now?"

He seemed excited. I rolled onto my back, giving him my belly. Yes, the cliche universal dog sign for trust and vulnerability.

"You want me to rub your belly, don't you?" he asked with a hint of amusement.

I let out a soft whine and looked at him pleadingly.

"I knew it." He chuckled. "My little one just wanted some belly rubs."

He rubbed my belly, scratching gently. I hated how much I loved it, my tail betraying me and thumped against the floor vigorously. He laughed a little harder at my reaction.

He continued to scratch at my belly and I relished every moment of it until… "You know, you aren't as frightening as you look."

I gave him a low growl both playful and a warning as my eyes narrowed at him.

"Oh, come on. You can't expect me to believe that growl."

Now he was asking for it. I scrambled to my feet and stood opposite him, growling as I took a defensive stance.

His eyes widened at my reaction. "No. We've been over this already Naphinae. You can't threaten me like that."

He was firm and gentle with me simultaneously. I let out a low warning growl, not backing down. I felt my muscles tense as I prepared myself to pounce.

He took a small step toward me. "Naphinae, you know better than to threaten me." He was still gentle as he spoke to me.

I growled again this time louder and with more defiance.

He took another step toward me, and my opportunity to tackle him slowly vanished. "Naphinae, I'm telling you, you can't keep threatening me." His tone became more commanding, his whole demeanor shifting.

I let out a low menacing growl, my fangs flashing in the moonlight. He took a firm stance as he took yet another step closer to me. His eyes locked on mine. "Naphinae, enough."

I took a threatening step forward, growling even louder, my hackles raised and ready to attack.

His eyes flashed with a mixture of anger and determination. "Naphinae, I've warned you."

My eyes widened in fear as his steps became harder, thumping against the floor as he approached me. I closed my eyes and whined as his hand clamped down around my muzzle. His grip was tight and firm, I couldn't pull away if I wanted to and I wanted to.

"I will not tolerate you threatening me again. Am I understood Naphinae?" He looked right into my eyes, his entire being was intimidating.

My tail tucked between my legs as I whimpered in submission.

He let me go and sighed. "Good girl, Naphinae."

I lay down on the floor and wrapped my paws over my snout, whining as the pain began to, painstakingly slowly, subside. He sat beside me and ran his hand over my fur.

"What's wrong little one? Are you hurt? Do you need me to get you anything?" The genuine concern was there, it was more than evident in his choice of tone.

I hopped up on the bed and curled up, still whining softly. He followed me and sat on the bed beside me.

"What's wrong?"

My tail curled around me as I continued to whine. He stroked my back.

"I know you're upset. But you need to talk to me. What's wrong?" He sounded more sympathetic.

I was more than ready to be in my human form again, just so I could punch him one good time, his grabbing my muzzle like that hurt like hell. He looked at me with understanding and crouched next to the bed. "I know this has been a lot for you, remember your strength." I did my best to do just that, I focused on my breathing and attempted to ground myself. He leaned closer to me, "I'm here for you little one, no matter what." I leaned on his words and leaned on the strength I didn't know I had, his strength. I felt my ears flatten against my head with the effort I was putting forth. He stroked my fur with a tender touch. "You're not alone."

I nuzzled against his comfort, and the searing pain started. The tidal waves of pain returned, drowning me in the endless void of agony. I whined as my breathing became labored.

He continued to stroke my fur. "It's okay Naphinae, just hold on to me. Focus on my touch."

My bones continued breaking and shifting back into place, every sound of a bone breaking was followed by an immediate whine.

He pulled me closer and he continued to do his best to comfort me. "It's okay, I've got you. You're almost there." His tone was as soft as his touch.

Every whimper and whine, every strangled cry, was a testament to the pain I felt as I surrendered to it. Every bone that broke sounded and felt more painful than the last.

"Just a little bit more. Come on Naphinae, you can do it." His encouragement meant more than he'd ever know.

The last of my bones broke and shifted back into their familiar alignment, my screams and cries subsiding. My body was left numb from the pain but trembling from the experience. He held me closer to him, running his hand through my hair.

"It's over, you made it through. How do you feel?" His concern was expressed through his expression, and his tone.

The way this man could flip through emotions like the pages of a book gave me whiplash worse than a car accident ever could. I tried to speak but my breath still hadn't returned to me. My tears were warm as they slipped down my face.

He wrapped his arms around my trembling body holding me with such love and such care. "It's okay, I know it was painful. You did it, you made it through your first shift. I am so proud of you little one."

For someone I had just met, his words brought me the comfort I never knew I needed. A level of understanding I didn't know existed. I pressed my face into his chest, every bone in my body rattling from the intensity of the shift.

He stroked my hair, his hand gliding through every strand with ease. "It's okay, you're safe now. Just hold onto me as long as you need okay?"

The amount of love emanating from Greyson was enough to make me weak in the knees, that was if I had the strength to stand.

I fell asleep in his arms; I didn't have the strength or the energy to fight against my exhaustion. Although I was asleep I could still feel him rubbing my back and I couldn't help but smile and snuggle further into his arms. The connection I felt with Greyson was like something out of a fairytale, surely there was a camera somewhere because there was no way this was real. Right?

Chapter Four

As I slept, little did I know he was making a quiet confession to me. A part of my subconscious heard him, but not being awake to hear his words made my heart ache in ways I couldn't describe if my life had depended on it.

As I gazed down upon her sleeping form, I ran my fingers through her hair. A strange and unusual feeling played at my heartstrings. I smiled as I looked down at her, my hand gently brushing through her blonde hair. Holding her in my arms, I felt instinctively protective over her, it was surreal. I watched over her. "Naphinae you look so peaceful when you sleep. I can't help but feel happy just looking at you."

She remained asleep, not a twitch or struggle. I continued to run my fingers through her hair and kept talking to her. "You know… I feel like I can tell you anything. There's just something about you that makes me feel comfortable and safe."

The words left me without a thought. What was this girl doing to me? As I spoke, she seemed to relax further into my arms. I couldn't tell if she was hearing me or not. "I know we just met little one, but I think I might be starting to develop feelings for you. Is that strange?"

I chuckled softly hearing myself speak, I sounded like a lovestruck idiot.

"I know it's probably too soon to feel this way given we just met today. But I can't help it. You're so beautiful, I could drown in those hazel eyes if you let me. Your personality is unlike any others I've seen. And then your tail is so adorable, it gives away your excitement."

As I spoke she smiled softly in her sleep, almost like a part of her could hear me even if it wasn't fully. My heart fluttered in my chest at the sight of her smile. "I've never felt this way about anyone before… And to be honest, I'm a little scared… But at the same time, it feels so right."

She cuddled closer to me, shaking slightly as she held onto me. I pulled her closer and wrapped us both in the blanket. "You're safe here Naphinae Kent. I won't let anything hurt you, ever." I spoke with conviction and the weight of my words carried. A silent promise I intended to keep.

I was in shock at how I was feeling, I couldn't grasp the concept of truly caring for another person. I rocked her in my arms. "Naphinae, can I ask you something?"

She muttered something so quietly that I didn't catch it. Her breathing remained deep and slow, the sound calming my nerves.

I leaned down and kissed her forehead. "Would you consider staying with me?" My voice was barely above a whisper, as much as I wanted an answer, the truth wasn't something I was used to and I was scared she'd say no. I was glad she was asleep. She couldn't see the vulnerability I hid from everyone. I'm the alpha, being vulnerable is weak. If it meant keeping her close then I would show every side of my vulnerability. I would wave it from the highest point on this planet.

I watched as she smiled, her face nestled against my chest. I chuckled softly and brushed a stray hair out of her face. "Naphinae, I don't know what it is about you, but I feel like I've known you forever. I feel like I can truly be myself with you." I felt myself smile at her. "I have a confession to make."

She didn't seem like she would wake up, her breathing remained calm and steady. I took a breath and spoke quietly, "Naphinae… I'm scared. I'm scared that if I get too attached to you, I might lose you."

She didn't move a muscle, remaining completely unaware of the weight of my words.

I felt my mask slip, my vulnerability shining through. "I don't want to be alone anymore. Please, stay with me. I need you. I can't stand the thought of being alone again."

Her breathing became a bit heavier, almost as if she was acknowledging my words. I was worried she'd heard me.

"Are you awake little one? Did you hear me?"

Her eyelids fluttered slightly, but she remained asleep. I stroked her hair and watched her eyes as she wrestled with her sleep.

"I need you Naphinae."

She muttered in her sleep, a small smile gracing her perfectly beautiful lips. I felt a twinge of hope.

"You feel it too, don't you? You're just as afraid as I am, aren't you?"

Her lips formed a brighter smile as she snuggled further into my embrace, it felt like she was subconsciously agreeing with me. I stroked her hair again, my heart warming at the sight of her smile. "I don't know what the future holds for us, but as long as we have each other... I know we can face anything."

Her hand almost instinctively found mine, our fingers interlaced. My heart melted completely. "Naphinae... I know you can't hear me right now. But I hope you can feel how much I care about you. You're special to me."

-NAPHINAE-

I woke up hours later to the sun peering through the windows. I sat up with a groan as I rubbed my eyes, only to realize I was alone in bed. I looked around the room and Greyson was nowhere in sight. I looked over and there was a piece of paper pinched under the lamp on the nightstand. I was both curious and worried as I reached for it. It was a note; 'Dearest Naphinae, I hope you had a good rest. Unfortunately, I have some important business to attend to. Please wait for me in our room. I'll return as soon as possible. With love and regret, Grey.' I held the note and immediately felt torn.

Waking up alone sucked more than I care to admit. Why did I feel so attached to him? As much as I wanted to listen and stay put, I wanted to explore. I wanted to see what my surroundings looked like. Everything was new and exciting, the sights, the sounds. I picked up the clothes from the floor, put on his shirt with my panties, and crawled back into bed for a nap. I decided to be good and behave.

After a few hours, the door opened. I sat up in the bed rubbing the sleep from my eyes. My eyes immediately darted over Greyson's appearance, and my jaw dropped. He was dressed in formal attire and looked absolutely stunning; this is the most handsome I've seen him so far. I was stunned, to say the least. If this was how he dressed for important business then I hope it happens more often. The smug asshole leaned against the doorframe, crossing his arms. The smirk that graced his face made me want to kneel before him and worship that perfect face. Safe to say, I was mentally smacking myself.

I felt my face heat up as I realized my jaw dropping was literal. I suddenly felt exposed under his gaze.

"W-What is it?" I stuttered out.

He stepped closer before speaking. "Oh, nothing much. I was just admiring how beautiful you look in my shirt." His voice was seductive, drawing me in more than I already was.

I nervously clutched the blanket, pulling it closer to me. I didn't know how to react. How the hell did he have this much power over me?

"T-Thanks…" I mumbled feeling like a bunny being stalked by a wolf.

He continued stepping closer, that gorgeous smirk still plastered on his face. "You're welcome. But the real question is… how does it feel to be wearing my shirt? Is it comfortable? Or are you just too distracted by my presence to focus on anything else?" his voice lowered, reeling me in further.

I couldn't bring myself to respond as my breath hitched in my throat. The small feeling of anxiety and excitement creeped in. He chuckled at my reaction, a sweet melody that only attracted me further. A dangerous calling sending a shiver down my spine. His laughter rang through my head.

"Y-Yeah, it's comfortable…" What was happening to me?

He came even closer to me, his smirk softening into a smile as he brushed a strand of hair behind my ear. My heart fluttered as I leaned into his touch.

His hand rested on my face and caressed my cheek. "So, are you ready for our date?"

My eyes widened. "D-Date?" I stuttered, suddenly feeling nervous. I had nothing to wear. I didn't even know we had a date planned, when did that become a thing?

"Yes, a date. I thought we could spend some time together and get to know each other better."

I took a deep breath trying to calm my nerves. "Yeah, that sounds… nice."

His smile got brighter. "Great. Let's get going then." He held his hand out to me.

"Greyson." I shifted a bit nervously.

He raised an eyebrow at me. "Yes little one?" His tone was still so attractive.

I broke my gaze at him and looked down at my hands. "I don't have anything to wear… and I don't think your shirt and my panties are exactly appropriate outside of the bedroom."

He chuckled softly. "Well, that's easily solved."

I looked back up at him and tilted my head. "How?"

His smile shifted to a mischievous grin. "Just come with me. I know just what to do."

He reached out, took my hand, and pulled me out from the bed. He led me toward the closet. I followed him, a bit hesitant but I felt excited too. As we walked into the closet I was more than sure my jaw dropped this time. The rack in the closet was wall-to-wall with elegant dresses on one side and suits on the other.

"Here we are. Just choose something you like." I felt his eyes roaming over me as he watched my every move.

I looked over the dresses feeling a bit overwhelmed by the variety of options.

He chuckled behind me. "Don't be shy. You can pick anything you want. And if you're having trouble deciding, I could always help you out," he said as he started leaning closer to me.

I felt a bit bold but I appreciated his offer of assistance. "What would you pick?"

He came closer to me and held my chin, making me look up at him. "Well, if I were picking, I'd choose something that compliments your beautiful body. Something that shows off your curves and accentuates your natural beauty." His hand moved from my chin, coming to rest on my cheek as his eyes roamed over my face almost studying my features.

I didn't let his subtle compliments rattle me as much as I was screaming inside. "And which one would that be?"

He smiled softly and spun me around, resting his hands on my shoulders. "That's easy. It would be the one in the back, on the far left." He pointed to a beautiful teal dress that would hug my body perfectly, while leaving little to the imagination.

I pulled the dress down and looked at him, "It's beautiful but… are you sure you want to give every other guy in the vicinity a show?"

His grin returned and a sense of confidence flashed across his eyes. "Well, maybe I want to show off a bit. After all, you are my mate."

I was immediately flattered by his choice of words. Someone give the man a prize. I felt my face heat up instantly. "Fine… let's just hope you don't end up fighting someone over me."

His laugh was intoxicating. "Oh, don't worry. I can handle myself. If anyone tries to lay a finger on you, they'll have to go through me first."

I pulled off his shirt and slipped the dress on. I stepped over and looked in the mirror, my eyes wandering over the dress against my figure. "Zip me up?" I flashed a smile back at him.

He stepped closer to me. "Sure thing."

He reached out, slowly zipping up the back of the dress. His fingers lingered tracing soothing circles against my back. I turned to face him, my heart fluttering at his touch. His hands rested on my cheeks brushing my hair back, slowly trailing down my curves. He looked down at me taking in every inch of the dress against my body.

"You look stunning in that dress." His hand came back up to cup my face as his other hand rested on my waist.

"You think so?" I smiled up at him feeling a bit self-conscious.

He returned my smile. "Absolutely. You look like a vision."

I smirked up at him. "A fight-worthy vision?"

He laughed softly, pulling me closer to him. "Well, I won't deny that I feel a little extra possessive of you now. But I promise, as long as you're with me, no one will touch you."

I pulled away and noticed all of the shoes he had. "Any ideas on which heels go best?"

He came up behind me and rested his hands on my hips. "Easy, those silver ones right there." He pointed out a strappy pair of heels sitting on the second shelf.

"The strappy ones?" I looked at him.

He nodded, running his hands over my hips. "Exactly. Those will look great with the dress. Now, let's see them on."

I sat down on the chair he had in the closet. "Help me put them on?"

He smiled at me and nodded; his eyes full of affection. "Of course little one." He grabbed the heels and came back over to me, kneeling and helping me with putting them on.

I giggled at the affection and care. "I'm beginning to think you enjoy this."

He grinned as he finished helping me with the heels. "Maybe I do." He helped me to my feet, stepping back and admiring how I looked.

"I would say, all it's missing is jewelry."

Without hesitation, he chuckled and stepped over to a jewelry box I hadn't noticed. It was a simple wooden box with carvings I couldn't make out. He pulled out a delicate silver necklace and came back around me, draping it around my neck.

I looked down at myself. I couldn't believe what I was wearing. "Wow... I don't think... I've ever looked this pretty." I looked up at him to see him already admiring me in a way I could only describe as an expression of pure love.

"You are always pretty little one. But tonight, you shine brighter than the stars." He smiled softly as he continued to look over my body and the way the dress clung to my every curve. The way he looked at me and his words in combination shot butterflies straight into my stomach. He stepped closer to me. "Well, what are we waiting for? Let's not waste any more time." He held out his hand in my direction, inviting me to take it.

I suddenly felt more excited and took his hand. "Lead the way handsome."

With a confident smirk, he wrapped his hand firmly around mine. "With pleasure my lady."

Chapter Five

I followed him out of the closet, my heels clicking against the hardwood floors. He led me through the hallway, his hand never leaving mine. I stopped for a moment to entwine our fingers. A gentle smile crossed his lips as he squeezed my hand lightly. "I love how your hand fits in mine. It feels like they were meant to be."

My heart skipped a beat as the word 'love' rolled off his tongue so easily. My face felt warmer at the thought as a rush of emotions hit me. "I couldn't agree more."

He pulled me closer to him and he leaned down to whisper in my ear, "And when I'm with you, everything feels right in the world."

I shook off the nerves and teased him. "Oh, I bet you say that to all the girls." I rolled my eyes with a chuckle.

He chuckled but his eyes reflected how serious his words were. "No, I don't. Because none of them have captured my heart like you have."

My mind went blank, the only thing echoing around was the word 'love.'

Is this what it's supposed to feel like? Is that what I'm feeling? I looked into his eyes as if searching for the answer to the question burning at my heart, the question that would rock me to my core. I wasn't ready for the answer. I couldn't shake the feeling, I had to know, I needed to. But what if his answer wasn't what I wanted to hear? What if it wasn't what my heart needed to hear?

-GREYSON-

I watched her smile fade and it made me nervous. Did I say the wrong thing? No… Was it too much too quick? She seemed lost in thought.

My concern grew, a knot twisting in my stomach. "Is something wrong? You seem distracted all of a sudden."

She didn't respond, she didn't even move, she just stared at me blankly. I brought my hand to her shoulder, the knot in my stomach tightening.

"Hey, are you alright?" I shook her gently, trying to get her attention.

"Huh?"

I let out a breath I didn't realize I was holding, but the worry remained. "You seem out of it."

She shook her head with a smile I could tell was forced. "Oh, it's nothing. Just thinking."

I tried to understand but I couldn't if she didn't tell me and I wasn't about to force her to talk to me. "Are you sure? You were staring off into space like you're somewhere else entirely." I wanted her to feel comfortable with me, and I could tell something was wrong.

"Yeah, I'm fine. Just lost in my thoughts is all." She continued to force a smile but it didn't reach her eyes, I knew it wasn't genuine.

"Is there anything I can do to help?" I tried to sound sympathetic, and I could feel my mask slipping.

"No, I'm okay, thank you though." She continued to keep up the fake smile and it was killing me.

I let a slightly frustrated sigh escape me. "Are you sure? There's no need to pretend around me little one."

Her gaze dropped to the floor, the fake smile dropping with it. "It's just… I'm overwhelmed by everything." She didn't look me in the eye when she spoke, something was wrong.

"Overwhelmed by what?" I didn't know if I wanted the answer for her or me. Was I what was overwhelming her?

She hesitated for a moment. "By my feelings for you…" She still didn't look me in the eye, and her voice was barely above a whisper.

"Your feelings for me?" My tone lost all confidence. I was many things and so far, okay wasn't one of them. My office was nearby and I squeezed her hand lightly and she allowed me to lead her there. I shut the door behind us and leaned against my desk as she sat in the chair in front of it. "Is it… overwhelming in a good way? Or… something else?" I wasn't sure I was ready for her answer, but I knew she needed to get it off her chest.

I watched her shift nervously in the chair, still refusing to look me in the eye. "I… I don't know." I gave her a moment to gather her thoughts. "It's like I've been looking for something or someone all my life, and then suddenly they're standing right in front of me… and I can't stop thinking about them."

I felt even more confused, I understood what she meant but… I guess I felt the same, I was just more sure in my understanding of it. "I see. So, you're having trouble understanding your feelings for me?"

She nodded, still avoiding eye contact as she began to fidget with her nails. "Yes… it's like everything is so intense, and I'm scared of getting hurt… or hurting you."

It all suddenly made a little more sense. Her fear was what was driving her. "Ah, I see. Let me tell you something. Your feelings for me are not one-sided. I have been feeling the same way." I took a moment before continuing. "And, let me assure you, I am not afraid of getting hurt or hurting you. In fact, it would be my greatest pleasure to spend the rest of my life with you… That is if you'll have me."

A few moments passed in silence. It was becoming deafening. I couldn't tell what she was feeling. "Please tell me you aren't suggesting trying to skip from getting to know one another to being engaged?" She finally looked up at me. She looked confused and scared.

I smiled down at her trying to ease the tension. "I guess I was a bit hasty there."

She chuckled, finally seeming a bit lighter. "I'm sorry I didn't respond right away."

I smiled down at her and shook my head. "No need to apologize little one. I should be the one apologizing. It seems I may have overwhelmed you too much."

She looked back down at the floor. "It wasn't you per se." She looked nervous again.

I stepped forward and placed my hand under her chin. "Look at me little one."

Her beautiful golden hazel eyes hesitated but met my blue eyes with curiosity and fear.

"Hey, there's no need to be afraid. I promise you, no matter what happens between us, I will never hurt you. Okay?" I moved my hand from under her chin and brushed my fingers through her hair.

"I know, but it's just…" She took a moment before speaking again like she was trying to find the right words. "I'm scared of losing you."

I took a deep breath and crouched down in front of her. "I understand how you feel. Trust me, I'm scared of losing you too. But let me ask you something…"

She nodded, her eyes fixated on mine. In any other moment… I wouldn't have hesitated to switch the mood, but this wasn't the right moment. "If you could have the perfect mate, would they be perfect for you in every way? Would they make you feel safe and loved? Would they take care of your every need?"

She seemed taken back by my questions. "My… perfect mate?"

I nodded. "Yes little one. Would they be the one person who makes you forget about all of your worries and fears? The one person who makes your heart race with excitement every time you see them? The one person who makes you feel like everything is going to be okay no matter what happens?"

She looked back at the ground for a moment, taking her time to find her strength to answer. "As much as all of that is important… I don't think that's what would make them perfect." Her voice was soft, quiet.

"Then what would?" I raised an eyebrow genuinely intrigued.

She really cared about her answer. She took her time to find her voice. "They would make mistakes as much as any person.. but backing down isn't in their nature… and when they do… they aren't afraid of being vulnerable, even if it's only with me… being a mate is sacrifice, it's a connection… a… a bond… it's feeling everything so deeply that it rocks you to your very core…" She didn't seem too sure of herself, but her vulnerability shined like nothing I'd ever seen.

I nodded at her answer, I agreed fully. "And would this person also be someone who you can trust implicitly?"

She shook her head without hesitation. "Trust isn't just given, it's earned. No bond can change that."

I smiled at her choice of words, the way she spoke, and the way her tone reflected how sure she was. It was enough to make me want her by my side forever. Despite her nerves, she was perfect. "I see. And if someone was able to earn your trust, would they be worthy of the role of your mate?" I was interested to see how she'd respond.

She shook her head again. "Trust is important no matter the relationship, not just for mates." She was gaining her confidence as the conversation continued.

I agreed with her, she made amazing points. Enough to render my attempts to show her I'm worthy, almost useless.

"True, trust is a major foundation to any relationship. Then let me ask this…" She looked at me waiting for the next question like this was a game show and she was dying to press the buzzer.

"If someone was able to earn your trust, would they be able to protect you? Not just physically, but emotionally and mentally? Would they be the one person you could turn to when the world feels like too much?"

Her entire demeanor shifted. "I'm sorry, I don't think I understand." She looked up at me like she was searching for a reaction. "What exactly are you asking me Greyson?"

-NAPHINAE-

This conversation was conflicting. I felt the need to tell him the reason behind my fear of feeling the way I do, but he wasn't giving me a proper opportunity. He sighed and rubbed the bridge of his nose. "You're right, I'm not explaining this well."

I stood to my feet and took control over the conversation. "Let me ask you a question this time."

He tilted his head and nodded; his eyes filled with curiosity. "Sure, what is it?"

I took a moment before deciding if the question was right. "Are you the alpha of this pack?" I did my best to sound stern with him.

His gaze flashed with confidence. "Yes, I am."

I placed my hands on his shoulders as I looked directly into his eyes. "Then why are you questioning your place in my life?"

He looked like his breath hitched, and his confidence fell away. "I… I just… I don't want to mess things up. And I know that in order to be a good mate, I have to trust you with everything. And what if you break that trust?"

I felt tears well up in my eyes. I let him go and turned away trying to hide my pain. "You think I would do that?" A silence fell over the room and I couldn't bring myself to look back at him.

"No… I don't. But the possibility is still there, isn't it." His voice was filled with remorse.

"My fear… It isn't based on my trust in you. I know in my heart you wouldn't break my trust. You have my trust completely Greyson." This was it, the moment I tell him why I felt afraid of loving him.

I could feel his frustration growing by the second. "Then what is it based on? What's stopping you from accepting me as your mate?"

I turned back to face him, my gaze shifting between him and the floor. "It isn't that I don't accept you, it's…" I was having a hard time getting the words out, tears blurring my vision.

He stepped closer to me, his hand gently cupping my face making me look at him. "It's what?"

I tried to compose myself. I failed miserably. "Growing up… I was the outcast of the Crimson Moon Pack. My own parents shunned me, my parents… The very people who brought me into this world, the ones who were supposed to love me without question. I gave them everything I had, there was nothing I didn't excel at… I just wanted them to be proud of me…" I paused for a moment feeling a lump form in my throat.

"All my siblings got their wolves, their first shift. Years passed.. 14, nothing, 15, nothing, 16, my parents grew impatient with me. I became an abomination to my own pack and it wasn't just my parents who started to treat me poorly, it was at that point the disgust of my mere presence poisoned the love everyone ever felt for me. When I turned 20 I was on my own, by 22 everyone abandoned me no matter how kind I was, no matter what I did to prove my worth. In front of the entire pack, my parents disowned me and banished me to never return to the place I had called home my entire life." I couldn't fight my tears anymore and despite my best efforts, they fell defiantly.

His eyes reflected my sadness, a silent understanding forming between us. I knew he listened. I knew he heard what I said. I wiped my tears and attempted to stand in front of him with confidence. "I am not afraid of what I feel because I don't think you feel it too... I'm afraid... because I can't take another person loving me temporarily."

He broke the connection our eyes shared and looked down at the floor, the sadness in his eyes deepening. "I see." His voice was quiet, unreadable.

"I guess what I'm trying to say is... that I have never felt this way about someone before... I'm afraid you'll see my flaws and realize that I'm not worth your time... I'm afraid that we'll fall apart..." I didn't know what else to say and I turned away from him. I couldn't look at him. The thoughts racing through my mind were becoming too much.

"I understand your fears little one. But I want to assure you of this at the very least. No matter how flawed you might think you are, it does not change the way I feel about you. And just because we may have our ups and downs like any other couple doesn't mean our bond will ever be broken." His voice displayed his sympathy for me, but it felt like pity. His understanding didn't feel like it was that, understanding. It felt like an attempt but it wasn't what he was trying to convey I'm sure.

I looked into his eyes and saw the love that he was trying to show me. "I... I don't know what to say.. I never thought you would feel this way about me... I'm afraid I'II only disappoint you... I'm afraid I'll fail you..." my voice trailed off, my breath catching in my throat.

He stepped closer, pulling me into a comforting hug. "Don't worry about disappointing or failing me."

I wrapped my arms around him, grateful for his warmth and reassurance. "But what if I do?"

He smiled down at me reassuringly, stroking my hair softly. "No matter what happens, I will never see you as a failure or disappointment. We may make mistakes along the way, but that's part of being human.... or in our case, wolf." He chuckled softly breaking the tension. "The important thing is that we work through those mistakes together. And even when things seem hopeless.... we always have each other to fall back on."

I leaned my head against his chest, my tears starting to fall against my best attempt not to. He rubbed my back soothingly, trying to bring me comfort as he held me tighter against him. "Hey now little one, don't cry. Everything is going to be alright."

I sniffled trying to wrestle my emotions. "But what if it's not?" My voice was strained.

He cradled my head in his hands. "Look at me little one." He waited for my eyes to meet his before he continued. "No matter what happens between us, I will always be there for you. And if you ever feel like you can't handle something on your own, you can always come to me for support. Okay?"

Unable to find my words, all I could manage was a nod.

He smiled softly at me. "There's my girl."

I giggled feeling the weight of the world lifting from me. He chuckled with me.

"Ah, there it is." He pressed a love-filled kiss to my forehead.

I couldn't help but laugh along with him. I wiped the tears from my face and he placed his hands on my face, gently caressing both of my cheeks with his thumbs.

"Are you feeling better now?"

I looked up at him. "Yes and no."

He raised an eyebrow. "What do you mean?" He sounded more concerned.

I took a deep breath. "The fear is still there, it's going to take time for me to shake it."

He nodded, and I watched as his eyes softened. "I understand. But I promise you, I will do everything in my power to make you feel loved and safe." He brushed my hair behind my ear. "You don't have to worry about anything. I'm here for you, okay?"

I nodded and leaned my head back against his chest as I took a deep breath. I wrapped my arms around him tightly. "Thank you, Greyson."

He hugged me against him tighter and rested his chin on the top of my head. "You're welcome little one."

I leaned into him feeling safe in his arms. He held me closer. "You know, I always thought that having a mate would be difficult. But now… I'm beginning to think that being in love isn't nearly as hard as we make it out to be."

There goes that word again… 'Love'… I changed the topic completely. "So, about that date… We aren't dressed this fancy for no reason."

He smiled down at me. "You're right. And what better way to celebrate our first date than by enjoying each other's company in a romantic setting?" He let me go and held out his hand. "Shall we?"

I smiled and took his hand, gripping it tightly. "Yes, we shall."

He led me out of his office, his pace confident and steady as we walked down the hallway. I couldn't help but admire him as we walked, his mere presence just exuded confidence and security. He turned his head toward me with a playful smile. "Are you checking me out little one?"

I looked away as I felt my face heat up, I knew I was blushing. "Maybe I am."

I could feel him looking at me. "You know… I don't mind. In fact…" He paused for a moment, making me look at him due to the silence. "I kinda like it when you look at me like that."

I changed the subject again. "So where are you taking me?"

He squeezed my hand, looking at me with a kind smile. "Trust me little one. I have something very special planned for our first date."

I couldn't help but giggle. "Let me guess… a surprise?"

He chuckled. "Yes, you're right. I want to keep it a secret for the time being." He winked at me before looking forward again. He pulled my hand to rest on his forearm as we continued walking. "I can't wait to see the look on your face when we get there."

We passed numerous other pack members, all of them looking at me. I felt small. I wanted to disappear. He took notice of the looks I was receiving and placed his hand over mine. He looked at a few of the people staring at me and a low-toned growl escaped him. "Ignore them little one."

I tried to smile but the more everyone we passed looked at me the more self-conscious I felt. Greyson must've taken note of my discomfort.

He let his arm fall and my hand with it as he pulled me closer and wrapped his arm around my waist as we continued to walk. "You have nothing to be afraid of little one. You're perfect just the way you are, don't let anyone make you doubt that." He leaned in closer and placed a soft, tender, kiss against my cheek. I looked down at the floor as we walked, trying to avoid the gaze of the others we passed. "Don't worry, I'll protect you." He pulled me closer. I looked back up at him and gave him a shy smile. He smiled back. "You're my mate now."

We kept walking and I noticed three females walk into the pack house. They were all wearing workout attire. One of the females approached us, practically ignoring my existence. She stood about three inches taller than me. She was gorgeous, even with what I was wearing… She made me feel like I was wearing a potato sack.

"Hi, alpha." Her tone was nothing short of flirtatious.

"Hello, Ashley." His tone was detached but he nodded politely. She looked directly at me with both disgust and disdain. I watched from the corner of my eye as his face went from civil and respectful to defensive as he scowled at her momentarily. "Ashley, this is my mate."

His words rattled her as she tore her eyes from mine. "But Grey, I thought I was going to be your Luna."

He took a more authoritative stance. "Ashley, we've been over this before," he spoke calmly but his words were firm.

"I-I'm sorry, Luna?" I was confused.

He turned to me and his expression softened slightly. "Ashley is one of the betas in our pack. In a wolf pack, the alpha is always male and the luna is always female."

Although he explained I was still confused. "What is the role of luna?" As the words left my lips Ashley looked at me with a hatred but the disgust still remained.

Greyson smiled at my interest to know more. "Well, to put it simply, the luna is the alpha's partner and the pack's second in command."

My mind immediately started racing. If Greyson is the alpha and I'm his mate… Am I his luna?

Before I could ask any more questions, Ashley kept whining about the unfairness of it all. Greyson began to look angry but his tone remained firm. "Ashley, enough."

Ashley narrowed her eyes at Greyson, she was clearly unhappy with his response. Greyson's gaze hardened at her defiance. "Ashley, leave." His voice was commanding and unforgiving.

She turned to me, her anger more than evident. "I challenge you Naphinae, for the title of Luna in the Wind Walker Pack."

Greyson stepped between us and looked down at Ashely. "Ashley, enough. You will not challenge my mate, and I will not tolerate your behavior any further." He remained calm and spoke with conviction.

"It's pack law, she has to accept my challenge or be banished." She seemed proud of herself.

He stepped closer to her and his entire being shifted. "You may be a beta, but that does not mean you can disrespect me or my mate. Now… LEAVE."

I placed my hand on his shoulder and I felt him relax under my touch. "If it's pack law then I have to… It's okay." I stepped beside him, my hand not moving from his shoulder. "Someone has to teach this bitch some manners." I looked her dead in the eyes as the words left my lips. She was stunned but it was immediately replaced by anger. What did I just get myself into?

He turned his head, looking down at me. A subtle hint of concern in his eyes. "Little one, are you sure about this?"

I turned my head to face him. "I'm sure. It's not just pack law, it's what I want." I gave him a soft smile.

He nodded slowly, pride flashing in his eyes. "Very well then little one."

Chapter Six

About an hour or so passed and I felt anxious, not for the fight with Ashley but for having to postpone my first date with Greyson. I changed out of the fancy dress and heels and put on something more fitting for a fight. Greyson gave me a sports bra and pair of tights that were obviously bought with me in mind. They still had their tags and they fit me perfectly. They were black mainly but had blue features.

"I'm sorry about having to postpone our first date, I feel bad." My words were genuine, I really didn't want to disappoint him.

He was sat on the edge of the bed. "It's alright little one." I knew a part of him was disappointed, I could feel it.

I paced back and forth in the room, my every nerve standing on end. I was unprepared for a fight in any form, human or wolf. I had no idea what to expect. Do I shift? Do I not?

He patted the bed, the empty space next to him, snapping me from my nervous thoughts. "Here, sit down." His voice was soft and encouraging but commanding all at once.

I sat next to him shaking out my hands nervously. "This is crazy, I'm not sure I can do this." I could hear my own voice trembling.

He wrapped an arm around me. "You'll be fine little one. It's all about being in control of your emotions. You must stay calm and focused on the task at hand. And most importantly…" He paused giving me a small smile. "You must not underestimate your opponent. No matter how much of a challenge Ashley may seem, she is still a beta in our pack. Betas are always weaker than alphas. Ashley has undergone training for years. She will have slight advantage in that. However, you Naphinae have an alpha for a mate. You can lean on my strength little one." He ran a hand through my hair as he continued. "Do you understand?"

I nodded. This much I understood but there was so much I didn't.

He leaned in and kissed my cheek. "I have faith in you." His breath tickled against my skin sending a shiver down my spine.

I took a moment to gather my thoughts, a moment to prepare myself. "Are challenges usually in human form or wolf form?" I looked him in the eye trying to show no fear. I accepted the challenge, fear wasn't something I should feel right now. I did this.

He took a moment, thinking about how to answer my question. "Both. Challenges are held in both human and wolf form, but the winner is the one that wins in their respective form. For example, if Ashley challenged you to a fight in wolf form, and you were to win... she would then be forced to transform back into human form and face you again until she either wins or submits."

I listened intently taking in his words. "So if it starts in human form it ends in wolf form?"

He simply nodded.

I had a burning question and there was no time like the present to ask. "If I win... when, when I win... does that mean I'll officially carry the title of luna to the pack?" My nerves crept back in waiting for his answer.

He smiled warmly. "Yes, that's correct. If you win, then the title of Luna will be passed to you and Ashley will be banished from the pack."

It hit me like a ton of bricks, everything that I knew I needed to do and say clicked into place. I stood to my feet. "Let's get this over with then."

He stood up and smirked, although he had a smug hint of pride in his expression. "I look forward to watching you in action."

I nodded. "After you alpha." I heard how it sounded after I said it, it came out a lot more teasingly than I meant it to.

He took no offense and responded right away. "As you wish my little luna."

I followed him out of the room, shaking my head with a genuine smile on my face as he led me to the main clearing.

He walked beside me, his voice becoming more confident as he spoke. "So, Ashley has always been a bit of a troublemaker. She's never been satisfied with the fact that she's not alpha, and she's constantly trying to challenge me and win the title for herself." He paused, his tone becoming softer. "But this time, she's chosen you as her opponent... which I believe is just her way of proving that she deserves to be luna over you."

I took in his words, they left a horrid taste in my mouth. "Why me though?"

He shrugged. "Perhaps it's because she knows I care about you and would never let anything happen to you. Maybe she believes that if she can defeat you, then she will prove herself worthy of becoming an my luna. Or maybe..." He trailed off, his voice becoming more playful as he spoke, "...she's just jealous."

That was enough to make me break, I couldn't contain my laughter. "So, she has daddy issues?"

He chuckled, his tone becoming more lighthearted. "Well, I wouldn't go that far. But Ashley does seem to have a bit of an obsession with me... and she doesn't take it too well when I reject her advances."

A low growl came from me, a pang of jealousy stinging at my heart.

His hand brushed my cheek softly. "Little one, I am yours and yours alone."

I nodded. I was more than ready for this fight now.

Our footsteps echoed as we crossed the clearing. As we approached, it seemed like the entire pack was there. Some were shifted into their wolf forms and others remained human. I stood in the center of the clearing and Ashley stood opposite me. Greyson stood beside me, his voice becoming more authoritative. "Ashley, you have challenged my mate and I will not tolerate such an act. You are hereby exiled from this pack." His eyes narrowed at Ashley, his tone becoming slightly threatening. "Do you submit?"

Ashley scoffed and shook her head. "Not a chance."

His tone became firmer. "Then prepare to fight."

Ashley let out a loud roar as she began to transform, her wolf form taking shape before our eyes.

Something in me enjoyed the idea of wanting to tear this bitch to absolute shreds, but I pushed it down and reminded myself of what my plan was. I followed suit and shifted into my wolf form, stifling my screams and whimpers as every bone in my body broke and shifted into its new alignment. This was only my second shift… So I did what Greyson taught me and grounded myself, not to him, but to my anger.

He took a step back, his tone becoming more cautious as he spoke. "Be careful, little one. This is Ashley's territory and she knows it like the back of her paw. She'll be trying to take advantage of your unfamiliarity with the surroundings to her advantage." He gave me a quick nod. "So be ready for anything, understood?"

I howled in response. I was more than ready for this.

He smiled proudly at me, his voice becoming more playful. "That's the spirit, little one."

Ashley let out a loud snarl as she charged towards me, her paws kicking up dirt and debris in her wake. I growled in response and dodged to the side baring my fangs. Ashley growled in frustration, her paws slamming to the ground as she quickly spun around to face me again. I didn't give her a moment to catch her bearing and bolted toward her. I felt my claws digging into the dirt beneath me, my speed was nothing like what I thought it would be.

"That's it little one! Keep up the pressure."

I could hear how proud he was, but now wasn't the time. I had to focus. I slammed into Ashley, sending both of us tumbling. I got to my feet, recovering quicker than Ashley. She landed harder than I did and I used that to my advantage and pinned her down. I growled at her, pressing my claws into her shoulders before snapping my jaw near her neck.

I heard Greyson start moving toward us but didn't move my gaze from Ashley. "Ashley, submit!"

I waited patiently for her submission, but Ashley was playing the long game. She waited for Greyson to get closer and attempted to bite him, I clamped down on her neck before she got the chance.

Greyson jumped back narrowly avoiding her attempt to attack him. "Well done little one!" His voice was filled with pride.

I didn't let up on Ashley and something about her struggling beneath me, made me feel powerful. She managed to get out from under me, taking me by complete surprise. "Little one, you need to subdue her quickly. She's a beta and she clearly isn't going to submit willingly." His warning was all I needed.

I growled lowly keeping my focus on Ashley. I heard him step closer. "Little one snap out of it. You need to take her down and put an end to this fight." His tone was stern but not enough to derail my focus.

Ashley suddenly charged at me, she was going to try and knock me over and I knew it. I let her knock me down so she would think she had the upper hand. Ashley lunged forward, attempting to pin me down. I let it happen. Ashley held me down and she thought she was victorious. She was about to howl but I clamped down on one of her front legs, the only sound that came from her was a whine. Ashley tried to pull away but I held firmly, not letting her go. Ashley whimpered in pain as she tried to free her leg from my jaw. I growled deeply as I let her go and pinned her down on her back.

"Little one, let her go. You've made your point and you need to put an end to this now," Greyson commanded from the sidelines.

Ashley let out a whimper as she struggled beneath me, looking over at Greyson in pure fear. I lowered my snout closer to her and snarled waiting for her submission. "Little one, don't make me tell you again. Let. Her. Go." His voice was more forceful as he spoke.

Ashley let out a whine of fear and bowed her head slightly signaling her submission. I let her go and backed up but not before I growled one last time to make sure my point got across clearly.

Ashley scrambled to her feet, trembling the entire time. I narrowed my eyes at her and growled again. Greyson stepped in her path. Protecting her? "That's enough little one. It's over."

I saw Ashely bolt after giving me one last look. She ran away as fast as her legs could carry her. Seeing Greyson step in the way in her defense… My blood boiled. My eyes darted between where she was and him. I snarled at him.

Why was he protecting her?

He looked directly at me. "She may have been disrespectful and aggressive towards you, but she is still part of our pack. And as the Alpha, I cannot allow anyone to harm another member of my pack without consequences."

I understood but my anger was clouding my judgement. I growled lowly, she didn't deserve his protection.

He sighed softly. "Look little one."

I could hear the disappointment in his tone, it broke something in me. My anxiety crept in again, the sound of his disappointment triggering all of my childhood trauma. He must've noticed the effect his tone had on me.

"Little one?" His voice was more concerned than anything else. I couldn't break not here in front of the whole pack.

Chapter Seven

I bolted. I ran as fast as my paws would let me.

"Naphinae! Wait!" I could hear Greyson trying to chase me.

My claws dug into the ground pushing me faster. I didn't stop until I reached the sanctuary of the bedroom I'd been staying in with Him. I used my snout to close the door but couldn't lock it. I sat in the corner of the room and focused on shifting back but it was like I was blocked. I heard the door open and I knew it was him.

"Little one?"

I didn't make a sound but he noticed me nonetheless.

He came over approaching me slowly and knelt next to me. "Little one what's wrong?"

I couldn't bring myself to look at him, the disappointment he had even if it was for a moment haunted my thoughts. He rested his hand on my shoulder but I was so out of it I didn't feel it.

"I know you're upset with me right now, but please understand that I had to protect Ashley."

I don't know if it hurt more that he thought my issue was his rules and his sticking to them or that he quickly forgot one of my greatest fears this quickly. He took notice of my discomfort and removed his hand from my shoulder.

I kept trying to shift back but I couldn't.

"I know it's hard, but you can do this."

I tried to focus on my emotions like I did to shift into my wolf form. It wasn't working. I didn't feel anything other than fear. I could still hear the disappointment lingering in his voice.

He moved to sit in front of me. "I know it's hard Naphinae. I believe in you, and I know you can do this."

I tried to focus less on what I was feeling now and tried to focus on my first shift, on how it felt to have his guidance, his care, and his kindness. I anchored myself to it desperately. My bones started breaking and I showed no reaction to the pain, the pain in my heart was more unbearable than the physical pain of the shift.

He didn't reach out to touch me but he moved closer. "Are you okay?" He seemed worried his voice full of concern, but all I could hear was the disappointment he had in the clearing.

I looked away from him. I couldn't bring myself to see the look on his face. I didn't want to see the disappointment in his eyes the way I heard it in his words.

He grabbed my chin and gently tilted my head to make me look at him, but my eyes didn't meet his. "Little one, please… I'm sorry if I hurt you." He sounded sincere like his words were genuine. He tried to catch my gaze. "Please understand."

Did he really think I was upset about him protecting her? I was but that wasn't what had me feeling the way I was.

I finally looked at him. As much as I didn't want to see the disappointment on his face, I needed to. He smiled.

"I'm sorry for the way I reacted earlier. It was a mistake on my part and you did nothing wrong." He moved his hand from my chin and took my hand in his. I looked down at our hands. He knew? He squeezed my hand gently. "Naphinae, you are far from a disappointment. You are an amazing and strong woman who I am proud to call my mate."

There wasn't a trace of disappointment in his voice, he was… tender? I could hear his words but I felt like a disappointment, I deserved it, it's what I am.

He noticed my pain and leaned in close, his tone becoming even more gentle as he spoke. "Please don't ever doubt yourself. I see so much potential in you and I believe that you can accomplish anything you set your mind to. You are not a disappointment, my love." His voice was filled with encouragement and affection. I closed my eyes and shook my head. He sighed softly, his voice becoming more solemn as he spoke. "Naphinae, I've seen the way you push yourself to the limit and give 110% in everything you face. It takes strength and courage to be able to do that, and you possess both of those things in abundance."

He gently pulled me close to him, his voice becoming more comforting as he continued speaking. "You are a worthy mate and an amazing woman. Never doubt that again, my love."

I didn't know what to say. That word came up again, 'love.' I felt tears well up in my eyes, clouding my vision as I looked at him. He wiped away my tears.

"I know it's hard, I couldn't begin to imagine, but you need to believe in yourself. You've come such a long way and I'm beyond proud of you." He smiled at me.

I was still conflicted, I felt like such a mess. I tried my damnedest to control my tears. He said I was strong and this felt like anything but strong. He pulled me into a tight hug.

"Cry if you need to little one." His voice was calm and soothing, and my tears wouldn't stop. "It's okay to let it out little one. Let all your emotions out, don't hold back." He rubbed my back gently as he tried to comfort me.

I cried for so long that I lost track of time. He continued to hold me, he never let me go as I drowned in my emotions. No matter what I cried over, he remained constant as he was determined to be with me through it. It took a long time and all the strength I had left in me to pull myself together to stop crying.

He slowly released me to look down at me. "Feeling better?"

I looked up at him and simply shook my head.

He sighed softly. "What can I do to make you feel better?" He sounded so kind, like I was the single most important thing to him, like me breaking, feeling broken, made him feel the same way.

"I'm sorry I disappointed you." I looked down as I spoke.

He lifted my chin, my eyes meeting his. "You didn't disappoint me little one. You're far from a disappointment." He kissed my cheek and smiled at me once he pulled away.

I looked at him and held his gaze. Something felt… different. He brushed a stray hair out of my face.

"What is it little one?" He looked at me intently, his broken blue eyes so full of concern but… they were also full of love.

'Love,' the word kept popping up. Is that what this is? Is that what I'm feeling? I swallowed the lump forming in my throat and looked away. I couldn't make sense of my thoughts.

He caressed my cheek. "Look at me little one. What is it?"

I closed my eyes and shook my head. "Please…" It was the only word I could bring myself to say. Please what? Please so many things… stop. Love me. Don't leave me. This is crazy! I met this man two days ago.

He pressed his forehead to mine. "I'm here for you Naphinae." I slowly opened my eyes and looked at him. "Please don't be afraid to tell me what you're feeling. I want to help you, but I can't if you don't tell me what the problem is."

I tried to speak, to say anything, but nothing came out. All I could do was shake my head.

"Please don't be afraid to tell me what you're feeling. I'm your mate, you can trust me with anything." He took my hand in his while he spoke, gently rubbing soothing circles on the back of my hand with his thumb.

I looked down at our hands and then back up at him. "I… I…" I took a deep and shaky breath before continuing. "I don't think I'm good enough." My voice was strained, and small.

His eyes went wide then softened. He brought my hand up to his lips and placed a gentle and loving kiss on it. "You are more than good enough."

Love… What is it? By definition, it's an intense feeling of deep affection. By my definition, it's fear. It's caring so deeply that it scares you. Love is sacrifice, it's smiling in the face of all your fear and moving forward together.

I looked into Greyson's beautiful broken blue eyes and sure enough, they reflected fear, but not the fear I felt. He didn't seem confused by his feelings. He knew what he wanted. I didn't break eye contact, it felt like I was searching for my answers in his eyes, but what was I looking for to begin with? He remained quiet and patient. I had no more tears left to cry. I wanted to curl up and just disappear, I couldn't take the weight of this uncertainty.

I sat up straight and looked directly at him, smiling in the face of my fear. "It feels like… every emotion I have is amplified. I don't know what to do with it. I'm scared."

He looked at me with understanding. "It's alright. You can be open with me, I'm here to support you. Your emotions are all valid and I understand that they can be overwhelming at times."

I had so much I wanted to say, so much I wanted to ask. I wasn't sure where to start. I felt frustrated. I stood to my feet, leaving him sitting on the floor. I threw myself onto the bed, covering my eyes with my arm. "I feel like I'm going crazy. I don't know how to deal with it." I sighed in pure frustration.

I could hear him stand up and start walking toward the bed. "Little one, please don't do this to yourself. Your emotions are normal and you just need to find a healthy way to express them." He pulled my arm away from my face.

I opened my eyes and looked at him, propping myself up on my elbows. "I don't know how to cope with this."

He knelt by the edge of the bed and I sat up to meet him halfway. "You don't have to figure it out alone. I'm here for you." He took my hand in his again.

I looked at him and felt unsure of myself. "What should I do?" I trusted his opinion more than I cared to admit, but this wasn't something I could handle alone.

"Let's start by talking about what's causing you to feel this way." He looked at me intently, like his singular goal was to make all my pain disappear.

I looked down, my eyes locked on my hand in his. My hand was so small in comparison to his. "My family never explained how pack life works. There are so many roles and rules… and I feel inferior."

He gently squeezed my hand, his voice becoming gentler and understanding as he spoke. "Little One, it's normal to feel overwhelmed when you're new to something." He smiled at me warmly, his tone filled with kindness. "But I want you to know that there is no such thing as feeling inferior. You are a strong and capable woman who has a lot to offer the pack. Your role is just as important as everyone else's."

I stared at him for a moment before finding my words. "I accepted the role of luna… but I have no idea what that means, no idea what I'm supposed to do. Let alone what the mate bond entails."

His voice became more soothing and encouraging as he spoke. "Little One, you don't need to worry about the details just yet. Right now, it's enough that you've accepted the role of luna. The rest will come with time and experience. And when it comes to the mate bond…it's a connection between two wolves that is deeper than anything else in this world."

I looked up at him, the words not coming to me.

The mate bond… I needed to know more. I needed to know if this was what was making me feel everything so deeply. I rubbed my hand over the mark he'd given me. "Is… is that what's making everything feel heightened? The mate bond?"

He nodded slightly, his voice filled with understanding. "Yes, the mate bond is a strong and powerful connection that can make even the smallest things feel amplified."

At least I knew I wasn't crazy. I felt my nerves starting to get the better of me. "Does it get better?"

He sighed and nodded. "Yes. it takes time to adjust to it, but eventually, you'll be able to control your emotions and not let them overwhelm you." He brought his free hand up and caressed my cheek lovingly. I closed my eyes and let his words sink in.

He smiled softly. "Don't worry. Everything will be alright. You're not alone in this, you have me and I'm here for you."

I moved a little closer to him, sitting more toward the edge of the bed. I patted the bed wanting him closer to me.

He moved to sit next to me on the bed. "What's on your mind little one?"

Boy, that's a loaded question. It may be easier to say what wasn't on my mind. "I know this isn't the most romantic setting… but I want to know more about you." I placed my hands in his and looked up at him intently.

His smile widened. "Ask away little one." He squeezed my hands slightly as he looked into my eyes.

I decided to start easy. "What's your favorite color?"

He chuckled slightly. "That's a good question. I have to say blue." He smiled warmly at me. "What about you? What's your favorite color?" He tilted his head waiting for my answer.

I smiled and replied without hesitation. "Green."

He chuckled again. "Ah, a fellow lover of nature's colors."

I nodded in agreement. Nature is beautiful and dangerous all rolled into one. What wasn't to love about the colors of the world? "Favorite flower?"

He thought for a moment. "Lily. And yours?"

I smiled and answered again with no hesitation. "Lotus flowers, the symbol of beauty through chaos."

His smile was so genuine. I made a silent promise to myself to make sure he kept that smile. "That's a good choice. The lotus flower isn't just beautiful but strong. It can grow in the most difficult of environments and still produce stunning flowers."

We talked for a while, getting to know each other a bit. I cleared my throat. "So, being luna…"

His smile remained. "What about it? Do you have any questions about being luna?"

I nodded and said simply, "Tell me everything I need to know."

He nodded and leaned in closer, his voice becoming gentler. "As luna, you'll be the second-in-command of the pack. You'll be responsible for leading the younger wolves and helping to keep order among the pack. You'll also be responsible for keeping the peace between wolves from other packs and making sure our territory stays safe. It's a very important role, but I believe you can handle it." He paused for a moment to think of something else to say. "Is there anything else you want to know?"

I thought for a moment. "How many others were offered the titled before you found me?"

He paused for a moment, his tone becoming more thoughtful. "There were a few others who were offered the position, but none of them were a good fit. You see, being Luna isn't just about having strength or power. It also requires intelligence, wisdom, and compassion." He looks at me intently, his tone becoming gentler. "I knew as soon as I met you that you had all those qualities and more."

I smiled. "Oh, you're only saying that because I'm your mate." I chuckled.

He smiled at me warmly, his voice becoming more reassuring. "I'm saying it because I genuinely believe you have all those qualities and more." He leaned in closer, his voice becoming more affectionate as he spoke. "And don't forget, we're bonded mates. That means that our connection goes beyond just love, it goes into the very core of who we are." He looked at me intently, his tone becoming more serious. "So believe me when I tell you that you were the only one for this job."

We had a silent moment of understanding, our eyes locked together.

I still had so many more questions. "The mate bond…What exactly is it?"

He smiled at me warmly, his voice was comforting. "The mate bond is a deep and powerful connection between two wolves that is formed when they first meet. It's like a spark that instantly ignites a flame, and it grows stronger as they spend more time together. It's an unbreakable bond that only grows stronger over time." He paused for a moment. "The mate bond is one of the most sacred and beautiful things in our world, and I'm lucky to have found you."

I felt my face flush. He's lucky to have found me? Those words made me melt.

I rubbed my hand over the bite mark he left on me again.

He grinned as he watched me. "That mark is a symbol of our connection little one."

I continued rubbing my hand over it. "It won't fade?"

He shook his head. "It will never fade little one."

I shifted nervously. "And what if your feelings change?" I swallowed the lump forming in my throat.

His smile faded slightly, and I couldn't help feeling like I said or did something wrong. He leaned in closer. "Do you truly believe I would ever leave you?"

My breath caught in my throat at the seriousness of his tone. "No… but people fall out of love." Did I just admit that's how I feel? Is it how I feel?

He shook his head again. "Love isn't just a feeling, it's a choice."

I nodded in agreement. "And what if you chose not to be with me?"

He sighed. "Then I would be the most foolish man in the world."

I could tell his words were genuine. I realized I was too in my head, to always follow the safe path. It was ingrained in who I was. Hearing him speak about his feelings, even if it was just scratching the surface, it was unlike anything I'd ever known.

I grabbed him by the collar of his black button-up shirt and kissed him. This wasn't heat, this was me, what I wanted, what I needed. He pulled back and grinned. "You're a tease, aren't you?"

I smirked up at him, my gaze challenging his. "Why don't we find out?" I pulled him in again, kissing him, but this time I adjusted how I was sitting and threw my leg over him, straddling his waist. He let out a low groan as he felt my weight on top of him. I smirked down at him, enjoying the power I held over him.

"Seems like you enjoyed that," I teased.

He groaned again and bit his lip, a smile on his face as he looked up at me. "I did…" He paused for a moment admiring my face. "Do you know what the best part of all this is?"

I shifted my weight and could feel him getting hard beneath me. "What's that?"

He groaned as I shifted, giving me even more power over him. He tried to get comfortable with me on top of him. "You're in my territory now, and there's nothing I can do about it."

I giggled. "You make it sound like a bad thing."

He grinned and rolled his eyes. "Well, for me it is."

I took a moment to debate my next move.

I pushed him down against the bed, my face inches from his. "Last I checked, I am not only your mate, but your luna. This is as much my territory as it is yours my alpha."

He looked up at me, his eyes wide with surprise. I have no idea where this confidence came from, but I hope it never leaves. My eyes were hungry as I traced the lines of his jaw, I lowered my face to his ear and lowered my voice to a whisper. "What's wrong, alpha?"

He shivered beneath me as he felt my breath against his ear. "I'm not used to having someone else take control like this…"

I could feel the power we had shift as I continued to overpower him with a confidence I never knew I had in me. I pressed my body against his and whispered in his ear again. "Looks like the big bad wolf has a weakness." I giggled teasingly.

He groaned and bit his lip as a slight blush spread across his cheeks. I watched from the corner of my eye, enjoying every second of him being flustered. "And what would that weakness be?"

I sat up slightly to see the look in his eyes as the next words left my lips. "As much as you are dominant, you enjoy being a submissive little thing."

He looked away from me, his face getting even redder. "I-I have no idea what you're talking about."

I chuckled and placed my hand under his chin, tilting his head to look back at me. "Oh? You have no clue?"

The power I was feeling was intoxicating.

He shivered slightly as his eyes met mine. I could feel him getting more turned on by the second. "No… I don't…"

I reached my hand down between us and palmed him through his pants, the texture felt soft and expensive but all I could feel was him enjoying the feeling of my hand more than I knew he'd ever admit. "Deny all you'd like, but your body betrays you alpha."

A loud gasp escaped him, his breathing getting heavier as my hand continued to move without restraint. "L-Little one…"

I leaned closer to him, my face inches from him again. "Yes, alpha?"

He groaned as his eyes stood locked on mine. "Do you want me to beg? Is that it?"

I giggled and pulled my hand away. "No, but I'm not opposed to it."

He let out a breath as my hand left him. "I won't beg for your touch." His tone was serious but I didn't let that sway my confidence.

I shrugged my shoulders and climbed off of him and the bed. "That's fine. But when that issue of yours becomes painful… Don't come crying to me." I walked into his bathroom and turned on the shower, starting to remove my clothes.

He let out a groan as he watched me walk away. "Come back here, you tease!" He tried to get up from the bed but failed because of how dizzy I'm sure he felt. He sat back down with a sigh, as I heard the bed creak softly beneath him and rubbed his head, his voice coming out muffled but just loud enough to be audible. "This is going to be a long week…"

I grabbed my phone and started playing music before stepping into the shower. I let the water run down and started to wash my hair.

He shouted over the music, "You're enjoying this, aren't you? The fact that you have me at your complete mercy… it must be quite the turn-on."

I giggled and rinsed my hair. "Wouldn't you like to know?"

He groaned loud enough for me to hear him. "I would very much like to know, you tease." I heard him grab his phone and wondered what he was doing but I didn't let it bother me. I continued my shower regardless.

I heard his phone. It sounded like he was making a phone call. I could've done something about him trying to ignore me but I let it go. "Hello?" He sounded bothered by something.

I lowered the music to get a better listen to his conversation but also to give him a bit of respect on his phone call.

He cleared his throat. "Uh, hi, it's Grey. Yeah, I know it's late."

I listened more intently as I kept showering.

"Listen, I know we're not supposed to mix business and personal, but I need your help."

I couldn't hear his choice of tone but I was starting not to like this. I was getting a nagging bad feeling. I focused on my shower and tuned out his conversation. I trusted him so I knew not to worry. His voice raised slightly and as much as I didn't want to listen, I'm glad I did. "Look, this isn't funny, alright? I'm not used to this. She's got me completely wrapped around her finger. And the worst part is… I like it."

I giggled to myself trying to keep quiet but I enjoyed the thought of him struggling because of me.

Chapter Eight

I heard the bedroom door open and close. I finished my shower and wrapped a towel around myself and came back out of the bathroom to an empty bedroom. Where the hell did he go? I took a deep breath and tried to clear my head. I stepped into the closet and put on one of his shirts and went through the stuff he happened to have for me. When did he even have the time to get all of this? I put on a pair of green laced panties and sat down on the bed for a while. I waited well over an hour and went back to the closet and put on a random pair of pants and slipped on my sneakers, grabbing one of his hoodies on my way out of the closet. I left the bedroom and tried to focus on his scent. The scent that started all of this… Home.

As I walked I kept telling myself this was okay, he could be doing anything. It was the anything part that bothered me. I started to get worried as I wandered the pack house, finding him being harder than I thought it would be. I followed the scent outside, suddenly feeling like this was an impossible task, he could be anywhere. I stepped out into the night and continued my search.

I suddenly felt a sharp pain, it radiated all over me. I pushed myself into a full sprint, running into the forest. The sound of my heart started pounding in my ears as I pushed myself, my desperation growing with each step. I got to the center of the forest and stopped dead in my tracks, I could hear him whimpering and my heart dropped the moment I realized it was him. My eyes darted around the darkness searching for any sign of him. I took a deep breath finding his scent again and took off racing through the dark of the forest frantically trying to find him. I pushed my body passed every limit running on pure adrenaline.

I knew not to call out for him, whatever happened could be more dangerous depending on how much sound I make. Should I shift? My body felt like it was going to give out from under me but I pushed passed my pain and focused. I kept running. Exhaustion was creeping in on me but I kept going. I needed to find him.

I finally reached a clearing, tears welling up in my eyes. A body on the floor, limp and hardly breathing. The smell of blood lingering in the air, mixing with the scent of home. I rushed over to him with one final push and kneeled beside him. His clothes were torn, his body covered in cuts and bruises. "Oh my god…" I placed my hand on his face, checking for any sign of life. "Grey…" I caressed his face gently.

He groaned slightly and his eyes fluttered open to meet mine. His eyes were filled with pain. "Wh-what happened?" His voice was weak and raspy.

"You're alive…" Tears streamed down my face as my voice trembled.

He reached up and wiped away my tears. "Yeah, I am… But you're crying. Why are you crying?"

I couldn't find my words. I was just so thankful he was okay. "You… You left… I waited. You didn't come back and I got worried, I left the pack house to find you… I got to the forest and felt pain and I knew it wasn't mine… I ran… I heard you whimpering and… and…" I couldn't fight my tears. "What happened to you Grey?" I felt like I was begging.

He looked away, his voice becoming distant. "I just…" He let out a frustrated sigh, looking back at me with sadness in his eyes. "You weren't acting like yourself, so I needed to get some space." His gaze became more intense. "But you followed me?"

Tears flowed down my cheeks uncontrollably. "I… I couldn't just let you go… I was afraid of losing you… I'm sorry, Grey. I didn't think… I was so scared… I'm so sorry." I cupped his cheeks in my hands. "I was scared I lost you."

He looked away again, his voice becoming soft. "You're so damn stubborn, you know that?" He paused and looked back at me, a faint blush spreading across his cheeks. "But I guess that's part of what I love about you." He took a deep breath and smiled at me.

"You…" I couldn't find my words.

He reached up caressing my cheek again. "You know what I'd like right now?" I tilted my head.

"What?" I couldn't deny my curiosity.

His voice lowered to a whisper. "Kiss me." His voice was demanding and full of desire. He groaned softly, his body twitching still obviously in pain.

I didn't hesitate, cupping his face in my hands. I kissed him deeply. He responded instantly. I could feel his heart racing. I pulled away, as sweet as this moment was… It would have to wait.

"Grey, you need to shift and get out of here." I turned my head, listening to our surroundings.

He gave me a confused look. "Shift? But… but I'm injured. I can't shift."

I shook my head, whatever was out there was getting closer. "You need to try, get back to the pack house."

He took a deep breath and closed his eyes. After a few moments, he opened them and looked at me with surprise in his expression. "I… I think I can shift." He stood up, his body twitching slightly as he prepared to shift. I kept an ear out for what was coming, preparing myself for anything.

His shift took a few moments but he handled it with ease. He stood on four legs and let out a deep howl, his gaze fixated on me. He moved closer to me as his tail wagged.

"Grey, get back to the pack house where it's safe." I ruffled the fur on top of his head and kissed his snout. I wanted to say it, I needed to, but this wasn't the time. Something was out there, and it certainly wasn't friendly.

He moved closer, nuzzling his snout against my hand. I wanted to enjoy this, it's the first time I've seen his wolf form. "Grey please," I begged him. It wasn't safe, he was hurt.

He looked at me with pleading eyes.

"It's not safe, you need to get out of here."

He whined softly and backed away. His tail lowered as his eyes replaced the pleading look they had with sadness.

"Go, I'll meet you at the pack house I promise," I spoke firmly, hoping he'd understand.

He looked at me for a moment, his entire stance full of hesitation.

After a few seconds, he took off into the forest completely disappearing from my sight.

I watched him leave, my heart weighing heavy in my chest. All I could do was cover him and hope he would get back to the pack house safely. I kept my ears up searching for what was out there. It was too dark to see anything but I couldn't hear whatever it was. I didn't dare to shift in case it was a group of hunters.

"Show yourself, coward!" I heard my voice echo off the trees.

I stood there ready to fight, scared or not. If whatever was out there hurt Greyson, the alpha, I knew I stood next to no chance. The sound started to get closer, but it didn't speak. I needed to be smart about this. If I run I risk putting the pack in danger, if I stay I might not make it back to Greyson. One life over many…

I stood my ground and waited, but it seemed like whatever was out there wasn't going to come out. I kept my wits about me and headed back toward the pack house slowly, not attracting attention to myself. As I got closer to the house, my adrenaline started to wear off and exhaustion started setting in. Just a few feet from the front door, I collapsed completely worn out.

-GREYSON-

After a few minutes, I made it back to the pack house. I shifted back into my human form and walked through the front doors. I looked around but I didn't see Naphinae anywhere. I sighed and walked down the hallway toward my bedroom, pausing as I passed the living room looking around again. I felt worried not knowing if she was alright. I got to my bedroom and lay down for a while, my chest twisted into a knot with worry for her safety. I shouldn't have left her alone.

I heard a thud outside and got up from the bed rushing to get outside. My heart was practically beating out of my chest. I ran up to the front door and when I opened it my heart dropped. Naphinae was on the ground, not moving.

I rushed over and practically fell to my knees beside her. "What…what happened?"

She didn't respond. She was unconscious.

I carefully picked her up and closed the door, bringing her inside. I laid her down on the couch and sat next to her. My heart was beating so loud it was all I could hear. "Please be okay…" I whispered. I didn't dare move my eyes from her, she looked exhausted. I ran my fingers through her hair, brushing the stray strands from her face. "Please wake up." I took a deep breath, praying she'd open her eyes.

I felt nothing but worry, I should've never left her alone. Not in the house and definitely not in the forest. What an idiot! I kissed her forehead and stroked the back of my hand against her cheek.

I tried to be patient. I could see she was visibly exhausted. I just couldn't calm myself down. "Please… Just open your eyes…" I pleaded with dead air.

I picked her up and carried her to the bedroom, gently laying her down. I covered her with the blanket and sat beside her, trying to keep calm as I waited for her to wake up.

Chapter Nine

I groaned as the sun shone through the window, picking up my hands and trying to block it out.

"Hey… you're awake. How are you feeling?" His voice was kind and full of concern.

"What happened? I don't remember getting into bed…" My voice was hoarse and my chest was killing me, the rest of my body was sore but not as bad as my chest.

He took my hand in his and smiled at me. His smile couldn't mask the worry he was feeling, it was written all over his face. "You collapsed outside the pack house last night. I carried you inside and put you in bed." He spoke slowly enough for my brain to process. I guess I was more exhausted than I thought.

I groaned and turned onto my side and cuddled against him. He wrapped his arms around me, pulling me closer to him. He kissed the top of my head and held me tightly taking a deep breath.

I could tell he was still worried about me. "Thanks for taking care of me." I couldn't fight how tired I still felt.

He stroked my hair. "Of course. I'm just glad you're okay." He stopped talking for a minute and looked down at me like he was looking for a sign I was hurt. "Are you in pain?"

I chuckled a bit breathlessly. "I feel like I got hit by a bus."

He chuckled softly and kissed my forehead. "It's probably just a few bruises and cuts. But don't worry, I'm here to take care of you." He paused for a moment and leaned back against the headboard, running his hand through his hair. "But I have to ask...why were you following me last night?"

I stopped for a moment, not sure how to answer his question. "I tried waiting for you after you left but…I had a bad feeling about why you hadn't come back." I remembered running through the forest trying to find him and tried to shake off the anxiety of remembering that was starting to creep in.

He was right next to me, he's okay.

He sighed and looked at me, his voice becoming more serious. "I'm sorry about that. I didn't mean to worry you." He took a deep breath, trying to remain calm. "But next time, please don't follow me when I leave. It could be dangerous."

I looked up at him confused. "That's even more of a reason I should follow you."

He sighed and shook his head again. "No, you shouldn't. If something feels off... then it means I need time to myself…. I appreciate you wanting to protect me, but this isn't the way to go about it."

I kept my eyes on him and started to feel a bit angry.

"No," I said, simply. "I'm your mate, you don't get that luxury anymore. Something felt off and I was right, when I found you, you were hurt."

The way he looked at me was like a challenge. "I appreciate that you care about me, but I need my space sometimes. If I want to be alone, then you need to respect that… Yes, something felt off and you were right, but you still shouldn't have followed me. It could have been dangerous."

I sighed. "I did give you space, I waited over an hour for you to come back."

"Yes, you did. And for that, I'm grateful. But following me when I need space... that's crossing the line." He paused for a moment and took another deep breath, trying to remain calm. "I know you mean well, but you can't treat me like a child. If I want to be alone, then it's your job to trust that I know what I need." He really had the nerve to be like this even though I was right to act on my instinct.

I was stunned. "And if it had been me that left?" I was starting to get irritated.

He looked at me surprised at the turn my tone was taking. "If it had been you that left, then I would've waited patiently for you to return.

I trust you, and I know you wouldn't leave without a good reason… But you need to understand, just because we're mates doesn't mean we can control one another."

I snapped completely, now I was mad. "I'm sorry? So waiting and something screaming at me that something was wrong… I'm just supposed to sit here?"

He rubbed his temples trying to keep a handle on his emotions. "No, I never said that. What I meant was… next time something feels wrong, you can tell me. You can let me know how you're feeling and we can talk about it." He took yet another deep breath, trying to remain calm despite the obvious irritation in his voice. "But following me when you don't trust me…that's crossing a line."

I sat up and my eyes widened as I looked at him. I wanted to shake him. I wanted to hit him.

I got up from the bed and walked over to the window. It hurt like hell to be on my feet but being next to him when he's assuming, when he's saying we can't control one another when that's exactly what he's trying to do… I couldn't do it.

"Where are you going?" He got up from the bed and walked up behind me, resting his hands on my shoulders. "Are you okay?"

I turned my head slightly, looking at him from the corner of my eye. "Just don't."

He furrowed his eyebrows. "Don't what?"

I turned to face him, I felt all my anger bubbling to the surface and I couldn't keep a lid on it. "Trust? Really? Do you think it was that simple? That I didn't trust you?"

He looked at me surprised, his voice becoming softer. "Of course I don't think that...I know you trust me. But I can't be around you every second of the day. When I need some space, I need some space. You can't control me… Look... I get it, okay? Something felt off last night and you just wanted to make sure that I was okay. But what if something had happened to you? What would have happened to us then?"

A low growl escaped me. "If something happened then at least we were together! Fucks sake! You want to talk about control? Just as much as I can't control when you need space… You can't control when I get worried… I passed out, not even making it inside because I was sprinting through the forest… looking for you!" I didn't care that I was yelling at him at this point.

He stared at me. I could see the anger he was trying to hide. "Okay, yes. You were worried about me and that's understandable. But you still don't get to make decisions for me! When I say I need space, it means that I need space." I could see his anger rising to the surface. "Look… I understand your concern and I appreciate it, but this is how things are between mates. We have different needs and we have to find a way to make it work."

I couldn't believe what I was hearing. "You didn't tell me anything! You just left!"

He rubbed his temples again. "I'm sorry, but I didn't tell you anything because I didn't want to worry you. Look, we can talk about this later. Right now, you should go back to bed and rest."

I could see the subtle hint of concern but the anger he had was still more than present.

I turned back to face the window. "Why, so you can leave again? So I can't follow you this time?"

He sighed, his voice becoming firmer. "No... because right now, you need to rest. You can't keep following me around like a lost puppy, okay?" He paused for a moment. "I'm not going anywhere right now, so you don't have to worry about that. But if you keep acting this way, then you might push me away... forever."

My heart sank. I shook my head, my mind started racing. I turned and pushed past him leaving the room without another word.

I walked out of the pack house needing to clear my head. I passed a variety of different pack members, some bowed their heads in respect and others glared at me. I didn't pay it any mind. I got outside and didn't stop walking until I found the lake. I could hear someone coming up behind me and I assumed it was Greyson.

"There you are…" I was right. "Listen… I know you're angry with me, but we need to talk about this. You can't keep following me around whenever you want. It's not healthy for either of us… Please, let's just go back to the pack house so we can talk about this like adults."

I scoffed at his words. "You're kidding right?" I didn't even look at him.

He sighed, trying to remain calm despite the irritation he was speaking with. "No, I'm not kidding. We need to talk about this now. You need to understand that I can't be around you every second of the day. When I need space, you need to give me space. That's how relationships work." He looked at me with concern as he spoke. "Please just…let's go back to the pack house so we can talk about this without causing a scene in front of other pack members."

I didn't give it a second thought, I was pissed. "You're a fucking hypocrite. Space? You didn't give me even a fraction of the time I gave you before you came looking for me. Trust? You say you'd never leave me but then threaten that I'd lose you forever if I didn't give you the fucking control you want." I kept my eyes on the water. I was afraid if I didn't I might actually hit him.

He sighed, his voice becoming sterner. "Listen to me. You can't keep comparing what happened last night to our entire relationship. Yes, I made a mistake by leaving without telling you, but I still needed space… And yes, trust is important in any relationship… but it goes both ways. If you want me to trust you then you need to respect my boundaries." He shot me a concerned look. "Please… just let's go back to the pack house so we can talk about this like adults."

I felt a low growl escape me as I held my head in my hands. "Go take a hike Greyson. I can't do this with you right now." Everything in me needed to be alone.

For the first time in the three days I've been here, I had such clarity in my emotions. Just for him to go and confuse me again.

"You know what? Fine. Do whatever you want… But just remember… if you keep acting this way, then it's going to push me away. And if that happens, then I won't be coming back for you. Think about what I said before you act on your emotions next time."

I didn't look at him, but I heard his feet against the gravel. He left. He actually left me standing there by the lake alone.

I felt my anger slowly start to fade, being replaced with sadness. A knot twisted in the pit of my stomach, solidifying with every passing moment I dwelled in how confused, scared, and hurt I was feeling. What happened to the sweet Greyson who wanted nothing more than to stand by my side? The man I almost told 'I love you' to, two days into being here. I hadn't realized it, but I had started crying. Standing there alone, with a beautiful scene in front of me, crying like a lovestruck idiot.

I could hear footsteps approaching but paid it no mind, assuming it was another pack member. I got tackled to the gravel beneath me.

"Hey!" I shouted.

"Hey! What's wrong? Why are you crying?"

I wiped my eyes and looked at the girl who tackled me briefly. "It's nothing…"

She had a sweet innocent smile, dark brown hair with bits of dark green highlighted through it, and lime green eyes. Her scent was sweet, like candy. "It's something if it's making you cry. What happened?" She seemed kind.

I looked back out at the lake and sat up. "I'm just having issues with Greyson… This mate thing is… a lot harder than I thought it'd be." I didn't realize how bad I needed to talk to someone.

She looked at me a bit confused. "You're having trouble with Grey? I thought you two were doing well. What happened?"

I looked at her again. "I don't think we've met?" I held out my hand. "I'm Naphinae. Naphinae Kent."

She took my hand and shook it. She had a firm grip but nothing that was disrespectful. "I'm Shade. You can call me Shade or Sade, whichever you prefer. It's nice to meet you Naphinae." Her smile was sweet, it brought me a sense of comfort I hadn't known I needed.

I kept my eyes on her, she suddenly looked a bit shocked. "Oh! You're Luna of the pack? That must be a big responsibility. How are you adjusting so far?"

I sighed and looked down at my hands. "Other than Ashley challenging me for my title, it's been okay. I haven't really done anything yet."

She seemed confused, at least her tone implied that. "Ashley challenged you? Isn't she mated to Tristan?"

There goes another name I'm not familiar with. "Who's Tristan?"

"Tristan is Ashley's mate. He's the second in command for the pack, below you and Grey."

I looked back up at her a bit shocked. "Oh… I guess I really need to familiarize myself with the other members in the pack, huh?" I felt myself smile and I laughed a bit.

She smiled back at me. "Maybe you do. It can be difficult keeping track of all the wolves in the pack. They have so many different names and roles, it's easy to get confused. Don't worry though, you'll learn quickly once you spend more time with them."

I felt a lot calmer now. "You seem nice Shade. Thanks for, umm… tackling me… I guess I didn't really want to be alone after all." I tried to smile but I still felt a little sad.

She giggled. "No problem. It's always nice to have a friend to talk to when things get tough."

I nodded. I completely agreed with her. "It really is… I've only been around Greyson since I've gotten here, but it seems like he's getting tired of me already." I looked back down at the ground. I really didn't want to keep crying but I could feel it coming.

"Oh no, why would he be getting tired of you? Has something happened between the two of you?"

I told her what happened, sparing no detail.

"I'm sorry to hear that. It sounds like there's been some miscommunication between the two of you. It might be helpful to sit down and have a conversation about what happened and how you can improve your communication in the future. It's important for the alpha and luna to be able to trust each other, and it seems like this incident has put a strain on that trust."

I didn't feel angry anymore, I just wanted this pain to stop. "But I do trust him shade. I just wish he'd see that I was only wanting to make sure he was okay." I looked down at my hands.

She put a comforting hand on my shoulder. "I know you do, and that shows how much you care about him. It sounds like Grey needs some time to process what happened, but hopefully, once he has had a chance to think things through, he will see your intentions were good and that you really do trust him.”

I sniffled and wiped my eyes. “Thank you, Shade.”

She smiled at me reassuringly. “You’re welcome Naphinae. Don’t worry, everything will work out in the end.”

I turned my head to look back out over the lake. “I certainly hope so.”

She leaned back against a nearby tree. “So have you done much exploring of the woods around the lake? There are some beautiful sights to see here.”

I chuckled and shook my head as I looked back over at her. “No, I haven’t exactly had the time.”

She laughed and let out a breath at the end. “I know what you mean, luna life can be busy and time-consuming… Well, if you ever get a chance, I would recommend exploring the woods. You’ll find some stunning views and hidden secrets that you never knew existed.”

I nodded and gave her a grateful smile. “I’ll certainly keep that in mind.”

She stood up and turned to leave, wiping gravel bits from her pants. “Well, I should probably head back to the pack now. It was nice meeting you, Naphinae. I hope we can talk again soon.”

I smiled still keeping my eyes out at the lake when I got an idea. I got to my feet and ran up to catch Shade before she got too far. “Hey, quick question.”

She stopped in her tracks and turned to face me. “Sure, what’s up?”

I took a moment to make sure I was asking the right questions. “What exactly is your role in the pack?”

Shade chuckled softly. “Oh, well I don’t really have an official role in the pack. My job is to assist with tasks that need to be done, like hunting or gathering food, or helping the elders with their chores. But mostly I just like to explore the woods and spend time in nature. It helps me clear my head and relax after a long day of work.”

I nodded as I listened and a smile spread across my face. “Well as luna, how would you like to be my second in command? Nothing too strenuous so you’ll still have time to yourself…. Just to help me adjust and settle?”

She blinked a few times as her eyes widened, I guess my question took her by complete surprise. "You… you want me to be your second in command?"

I simply nodded, keeping a small smile on my face.

Smiling widely, she nodded. "I would be honored to be your second in command, Naphinae. Thank you for trusting me with this responsibility. I promise that I will do my best to support and assist you in any way that I can."

I giggled a bit at her reaction. "Please, Naph is just fine."

She joined in, in my laughter. "Alright, Naph it is then."

Chapter Ten

After talking with Shade for a while, we parted ways and I walked back into the pack house. I needed to face the issues with Greyson head-on. I was still hurt by his assumptions but if this was going to work, Shade was right, we needed to communicate better. I passed a few pack members as I made my way to the kitchen. I decided to make something small to eat for both Greyson and I. Hopefully, Greyson would take to my gesture and we could talk without yelling.

I finished making some stuff to eat. Fruit salad, sandwiches, lemonade, and tea just in case he doesn't like lemonade. I walked into the bedroom we'd been sharing, struggling to get the door open with my arms full. "Grey, could you open the door please?" I tried to sound sweet but my heart was beating too loud.

He didn't come to the door. "I don't want to fight with you anymore Naphinae. Can we just talk about this later? Please… I need some space right now."

I looked at the door, I couldn't speak. I put the food and drinks I just made to enjoy with him in front of the door and walked away. I could feel it coming, I was about to break down.

I ran off as fast as my legs could carry me. I made it to the center of the clearing, in eyeshot of almost everyone. 'Not here. Please not here,' I pleaded with myself, my eyes tearing up and fast. My bones started to break and shift, screaming as every part of me was in pain.

My heart, my soul. I felt alone and iced out. I had nothing, I am nothing. I had no control over this shift, nothing to anchor to, to get through it. I fell to the floor, my tears falling without my consent as my bones continued to break, the sound echoing in the air mixing with my screams of agony.

I heard the sound of her screams and immediately ran outside to see her lying on the ground, her bones breaking as she continued to scream in agony.

"Oh my god…" I rushed over to her and knelt by her side. "Hey... hey, it's okay. It's going to be alright." I put my hand on her shoulder and stroked her hair, trying to reassure her. "Just take deep breaths, okay? Everything's going to be fine." I was concerned but did my best to push it down and focus on her. "You're not alone, I'm right here."

She coughed and continued to cry, her screams coming consistently every seven seconds followed by the breaking of another bone.

I stroked her hair trying to give her something to focus on, I winced at the sound of every break that sliced through the silence. "It's going to be okay, I promise. Just breathe… Breathe." I continued stroking her hair. "Look at me… look at me, okay? You're not alone. I'm here with you."

She opened her eyes. The pain was still very present and overwhelming her. I took her hand in mine. "I'm going to shift so that I can help you. It might hurt a little, but it'll be okay… Just try to relax. You don't have to do anything else." I kissed her forehead and stepped away from her.

I started my shift. It was anything near what she was feeling, I've shifted so many times I've lost count. The rush of power washed over me as I shifted quickly, my focus aimed toward helping Naphinae get through this. This was my fault, she was going through this because of me and I knew it. Running out of the bedroom, I saw the food she'd made. It must've taken her a while. I was such an ass and this wasn't going to be enough to make up for it.

I looked down at her, it was like her body was trying to reject her shift. Watching her go through this was torture.

She screamed and cried, silently pleading for it to stop. I lay down next to her and nuzzled my snout against her, I could feel her tension ease slightly. 'Just hold on a little longer little one.' I watched her agony continue. Her crying was breaking my heart and there wasn't much I could do, not even the mate bond could help her right now. Her shift was slow, probably the slowest I've seen her experience so far.

She whined and howled as she struggled to her feet. I stood up next to her and supported her weight against me. I nuzzled my head against her neck trying to comfort her as she struggled to catch her bearings.

She fell back down against the grass, she was unconscious. She looked completely worn out. I shifted back. I walked over to her still body and picked her up, cradling her against me. "There you go… I've got you. It's okay little one… Just rest now. Everything is going to be alright." I started walking back to the pack house, hoping she'd wake up soon.

After an hour there was a knock at the door, I reluctantly got up from the bed leaving Naphinae to rest and answered the door. It was Shade.

I looked down at her. "She's fine, she's just resting. She had a bad shift...she was in a lot of pain." I paused for a moment and took a deep breath, trying to remain calm. "But it's alright... she's okay now… I don't really have time to talk right now, can we do this later?" I started to close the door but Shade stopped me with her hand.

She didn't look at me but at Naphinae, looking at her as she rested. "Alpha, with all due respect. You need to get your shit together."

I looked down at her but her eyes challenged mine. "Excuse me?" I did my best to remain calm.

"You have no idea do you?" She didn't seem scared of me.

The irritation from earlier was still lingering and this wasn't helping. "No idea about what?" I huffed.

"She loves you. She loves you and you hurt her. She may not have said it, shit she may not even know. The way she cried when you left her by the lake and the way you are the only constant on her mind… she loves you, and you hurt her." Shade's eyes didn't leave mine, showing me I shouldn't doubt her words.

I sighed and rubbed my temples. "I know she loves me...that's not the problem. The problem is that she's acting like a child. She can't control her emotions...she thinks that if she just follows me around then I'll do whatever she wants." My voice became more insistent. "I can't spend my entire life dealing with her drama. It's exhausting."

Shade looked at me unimpressed. "If you really think that's why she follows you, then you're just as blind to her emotions as she is."

I looked down at Shade. "I'm sorry that she's upset, but I can't just drop everything I'm doing to comfort her." I paused for a moment and took a deep breath. "My pack needs me and if I can't focus on what they need then we're all going to get hurt. Do you understand?"

She nodded, but her emotion was unreadable. "I understand perfectly fine that you would much rather neglect your mate's feelings than help her understand them. She's new to this and it's obvious." Why was Shade doing this?

I sighed. "I'm not trying to neglect her feelings. I understand that she's new to this and I've been trying to be patient with her. But she can't expect me to drop everything every time she has a problem. Do you expect me to just stop leading the pack whenever she needs me? Because if so, then you clearly don't understand the responsibilities that come with being an alpha."

Shade simply shook her head. "There's a hierarchy for a reason. If you don't trust in your pack to help when you need it, then none of us will survive. You aren't as alone as you're forcing yourself to be. Instead, you command her like a dog and make her stay put when she has no one. If I hadn't found her earlier, she might have shifted sooner and she would've been alone." Shade sighed and rubbed the bridge of her nose. "You're right it isn't my business. Mark my words alpha, you keep this up and her pushing you away will be the least of your problems."

I stared at her, my gaze becoming more intense. "You're right... it's not your business. So why don't you just go back to your little hole and mind your own damn business? You have no idea what I'm going through right now, so don't act like you do. I don't need anyone telling me how to handle my pack... So until you can learn to respect that, just stay out of my way."

-NAPHINAE-

I woke up shifted back into my human form, I didn't even feel it happen. I must've been really exhausted. My attention on my body was snatched by the yelling at the door. Shade? Greyson? Why were they yelling? I heard him yelling at her and although I couldn't physically get my body to move, I could still say something. "Don't talk to her like that."

He turned and looked at me with an expression of pure anger. "What did you just say?"

I took a breath and it burned. "Don't talk to her like that. She's my beta. She's just looking out for me."

He rolled his eyes and sighed, his voice becoming more insistent as he spoke. "Oh please... don't play the victim here. You can't expect me to treat you with kid gloves just because you had a bad shift. I'm your alpha, and I won't tolerate insubordination from anyone. So either respect my authority or leave my pack. It's that simple."

I took a moment and nodded. I swallowed the lump in my throat and my eyes clashed with his. "Is that an order alpha?"

He stared at me, his eyes narrowing. "That's exactly what it is." His face showed no sign of any affection, the love he had was nonexistent. "Do you understand?" He looked at me with contempt as he waited for my response.

I forced myself up from the bed and struggled but got to Shade. She took my arm and allowed me to share my weight with her. I appreciated her friendship more than I could express right now. "That's right... lean on your beta. That's what you want, isn't it? For everyone to treat you like the helpless pup that you are." He huffed before he spoke again. "Well guess what... I'm not your babysitter. So either learn to stand on your own two feet or leave my pack because I don't have time for this."

His words cut into me but I somehow found the strength to stand up without assistance. "Shade, wait for me outside please." I kept my eyes on Greyson the entire time I spoke.

Shade did as I asked and left the pack house.

"Are you trying to challenge me? Because if you are then you're making a big mistake." He was clearly pissed, but I didn't care.

I stepped up to him… I smacked him, it hurt. His head snapped to the side as my hand made contact with his face. "To think I was ready to tell you I figured it out… figured out my feelings toward you… that I love you…. Is this who you really are?! A man who thinks I need him? Because the man I was falling in love with is nowhere in this house. The man who helped me through my first shift, the man who listened to my story and promised his feelings for me would never change!" I was hurt but I masked it with my anger.

He turned back to face me with a look of pure disbelief. "You… you're in love with me?" He took a moment to let it sink in. "Are you serious right now?" His eyes searched mine but he made no movement toward me or away from me.

"I have been here for three almost four days… I stood in this room and waited for you every time you asked… your pack is important to you and I understand that." My eyes started welling up with tears. "You've chosen them over what this could have been. I didn't follow you last night for any other reason than wanting to make sure you were safe, even if that meant putting myself in harm's way. I didn't care the cost, but it looks like the cost was you." My tears start streaming down my face.

He looked remorseful. "I'm sorry. I don't want to hurt you, but I can't just ignore my responsibilities as the alpha."

I looked down and shook my head willing myself not to cry. "I never asked you to Greyson… and that's what you're not seeing…" The truth was bitter and it hurt to say it all out loud.

"I love you too… but it doesn't change the fact that I have a pack who depends on me." His tone was firm, it didn't sound like he was registering anything I was saying.

"Don't say those words to me when they're nothing but an empty statement." My eyes snapped up to his.

"Do you want to know the truth?" He took a moment before speaking again. "I don't know what to do… I don't know how to balance being an alpha and being in a relationship with you."

He stared at me waiting for a response.

"You could've come to me the way you expected me to come to you… I may know nothing about being luna but I am more than willing to do it…" I wanted him to see and hear how much everything I was saying was true but it wasn't something I could force.

He rubbed his temples. "I know… I know. I'm sorry okay? I've been so focused on being an alpha that I never really thought about how my actions would affect you." His eyes softened. "Can you forgive me?"

"Greyson… you broke my heart before I could give it to you fully." My tears started falling faster but I choked back the urge to break any further. "I think I'm the one who needs time now."

He looked at me pleadingly. "Please, just listen to me for a second. We don't have to rush things. We can take our time… We can work through this together. I know I was distant, and that wasn't fair to you… but that doesn't mean I don't love you."

I wanted to believe him. I wanted those three words to mean something to him the way they did to me. "And that's what I wanted… but you've shown me a side to you that… I think you need to work on." I stood a little taller trying to gather myself. "This pack is more than willing to work together. You aren't letting them grow. You need to rely on the chain beneath you, I think you'll see a positive change in everyone including yourself if you were to do that."

He nodded and sighed. "You're right. I promise I'll do better… Can we start over?" His eyes remained fixed on mine, they were kind and gentle but I wasn't falling for it again.

"I need to go." I stepped out of the room and left the pack house finding Shade waiting for me just outside the front door. He followed me out a few steps behind me. "Hey shade, could you please talk to luna? I didn't mean for things to turn out this way."

Shade looked at me for a moment before turning to speak with Greyson. "I think you need to give her time alpha. I'm sure she'll come to you when she's ready… until then I'll show her what I can and she'll stay with me."

And with that said, she linked her arm with mine and we walked away without another word to or from Greyson.

Chapter Eleven

The following few days were the hardest. The mate bond kept pulling me toward Greyson as if my life depended on it. I could feel his mind in turmoil and it took every ounce of strength I had not to go to him.

Shade was kind and I learned a lot about her while I stood with her. We started my training as luna from the bottom. I got to know the elders, Delany, and Vincent. They're the oldest mates in the pack and from the looks of it, their bond is strong. It's like they can communicate by doing and saying nothing at all. I met Tristan and I have no idea how he ended up mated to a bitch like Ashley, but she made him happy. It wasn't my place to change that.

Amongst some of the other things I did. I helped in the kitchen with preparing dinner for the pack and learned a few pack favorites. In turn, I met another mated couple, Rowan and Cody Conri. They have two pups, Oakley who's 4, and Oliver who's 2. Both pups took a liking to me which I guess is a good sign.

I trained my ass off, shifting in and out of human form. I could almost shift at will with minimal pain. It was hard but it was worth it. I trained with Shade, as well as Ryker James, the gamma of the pack. Shade thought Ryker was her mate, but for someone so strong-willed, she was absolutely terrified to find out and be wrong. I saw more of the territory thanks to Shade. Her wolf was stunning. She was completely grey which helped her blend no matter the time of day, and her eyes remained their lime green color even in her wolf form.

I could say confidently the pack had taken well to me… and it felt like this was where I belonged. It wouldn't come without its challenges to help maintain the pack as their luna, but I looked forward to the challenge.

It'd been about two weeks since I'd been around Greyson directly and I was not sure I was ready to face him. If there was one thing I learned in the past weeks with Shade, I didn't give myself enough credit as far as the limits of my strength.

I had just finished training with Shade and Ryker when I decided to head into the pack house. There he was, Greyson freaking Carver. He was wearing a suit without the jacket, the sleeves to his burgundy button-up rolled up his arms. He had his hands in his pockets as he spoke with Tristan.

His eyes found mine and my heart nearly leapt from my chest. "Ah, little one… I didn't know you were in the house." He paused for a moment and shifted his stance nervously. "You look well. It's nice to see that you're settling in so well." He smiled at me, despite the tension that still lingered between us like a hidden veil.

"I didn't think anyone was home." I looked around nervously.

"Don't worry you aren't interrupting anything. I was just speaking with Tristan, why don't you come over and join us?" He gestured for me to join them as he chuckled at my nerves.

I approached him slowly, my heart racing as I felt the weight of the mate bond pulling me toward him. "I'm not interrupting anything?" I questioned, my voice wavering slightly.

He chuckled softly and shook his head. "No, you're not interrupting anything. We were just discussing the latest pack news… it's nothing you need to worry about." He gestured for me to take a seat next to him, his voice becoming gentler as he spoke. "Come sit… I want us to talk."

I hesitated for a moment, my eyes darting between Tristan and Greyson, before finally taking a seat beside Greyson. "Okay…" I said, my voice barely above a whisper.

He smiled and placed his arm around my shoulders. "Thank you… Can I ask you something?"

I felt my heart race as his arm wrapped around me, the familiar scent of cedar and sandalwood enveloping me. "Um… sure…" I replied nervously, my gaze fixed on the floor.

He took a deep breath. "I know this has been hard for you... the way I've treated you, and I just want you to know that I'm truly sorry for how things have been between us. Can you find it in your heart to forgive me little one?"

I took a deep breath, trying to steady my racing heart. "Greyson..." I began hesitantly, my voice barely above a whisper. "It's not just the way you've treated me...it's the way you've treated yourself."

He nodded his head slowly. "You're right... it's not just about you. I've been so focused on being an alpha that I forgot about my own needs... I let my insecurities get the best of me. I realize now that I need to let go of my fears and trust in those around me... including you, Naphinae."

"Greyson, I'm not sure this is a conversation we should be having in front of your beta." I tried to keep my composure but it was hard given everything that happened.

He nodded in understanding and looked at Tristan. "You're right... I'm sorry." His eyes darted from side to side as he continued to speak. "Could you please give us a minute?" He looked back at me, his voice becoming gentler as he spoke. "I want to make this right with you, Naphinae... no matter what it takes." His tone took on a more pleading quality. "Please... give me another chance."

I thought about it for a moment. A wicked grin crossed my face as I looked over at him. "Sure... one condition."

He raised an eyebrow. "One condition?" He seemed puzzled by my sudden courage. "What would that one condition be?"

I kept my mischievous smile as I spoke. "You have to earn it... Spar with me. Human form."

His eyes widened in surprise. "You want to spar with me? Why on Earth would I agree to that?" He seemed amused by the idea after a few moments on the thought. "You do realize that you're going to lose, right?"

I smirked. "I've been away from you for a couple of weeks. This will show you my progress as well as... as you say, express my feelings in a healthy way. And what better way then to kick your ass for all the emotional bullshit you put me through... alpha." I raised an eyebrow waiting for his response.

He chuckled softly. "Alright little one, I'll agree to your terms. But I want to make one thing clear… this fight is going to be short. You might have been away from me for a couple of weeks, but I haven't sat on my ass the whole time either." His tone shifted from amused to commanding, boy did that give me chills.

I pushed down the fact that he was turning me on with just his words and focused my emotional state on courage, of which I had plenty. "My, my. The big bad wolf just may be scared of his little luna." I gasped playfully wanting to rile him up.

He rolled his eyes and chuckled again. It was low and raspy. "Scared of you? Don't be ridiculous… I just want to make sure that you understand the level of our abilities. I won't be holding back because you're my mate. Do you understand?"

I nodded. I didn't dare speak although my smirk remained. The things he was doing to me with just his words were indescribable.

He smiled and placed his hand on my cheek. I felt like I was on fire, but it was bearable. "Good… Let's get this over with. I hope you're ready for this little one." His voice started to take a more taunting quality. "You're about to see just how strong your alpha is."

I stood to my feet and looked up at him, resting my hand on his chest. "Shall we?"

He grinned and nodded his head slowly, his voice becoming more amused as he spoke. "Let's." He paused for a moment trying to remain calm despite the excitement in his voice. "Don't hold back… give me all you got, luna." His tone took on a slightly challenging quality. "I want you to know exactly who you're dealing with here."

I giggled.

We made our way to the clearing and stood opposite each other. He took a deep breath and crouched down, his eyes darting back and forth as he spoke. "You ready, luna? This is your last chance to change your mind." He paused for a moment and took another deep breath, trying to remain calm despite the excitement in his voice. "I don't want to hurt you… so if you feel like this is too much… just say the word."

I shook my head, keeping my eyes on him. "Not a chance. I think you'll see I'm not the same helpless pup you broke two weeks ago."

He stood up straight, his voice becoming more confident. "Alright, luna... let's do this." His tone took on a slightly challenging quality. "Show me what you've learned while you were away but don't hold back... make your move and show me what you got."

I chuckled defiantly. "Now, now alpha. Age before beauty." I took a defensive stance, preparing myself for whatever he was going to do.

He laughed softly and shook his head. "You're definitely not the same Luna I remember... it's been a while since you've had such a witty retort." His tone took on a slightly challenging quality. "But make no mistake, luna... I will always be the alpha... age means nothing in this world." His eyes became narrowed and focused. "Show me what you can do."

I bowed playfully. "As you wish alpha."

I bolted out of sight, knowing he could still smell my scent left me at a disadvantage. I snuck up behind him and snaked my way up his back, tucking my arm beneath his chin and holding pressure around his neck. He smiled softly and glanced up at me. "That's more like it… but I see what you're trying to do, luna. You want to catch me off guard. That tactic won't work with me. I know you better than that... I can smell your scent from a mile away."

I giggled.

As if I didn't know that already. I focused the way Shade and Ryker taught me to, focusing on his strength and calling to it. Being the mate of the alpha had its perks and his strength was one of them. I tucked my legs around his waist and used his own weight against him, flipping us both over, and landing him on his stomach. I pinned him down and tucked his wrist between his shoulder blades behind his back using my weight to keep my hold.

He chuckled softly and shook his head. "Alright, luna... I'll give you this... that was impressive, but don't think you can take me by surprise like that again… You may be my mate but don't forget who your alpha is." He grinned and tried to push himself up off the ground, struggling against my weight.

"Concede and this'll be over." I pushed his wrist higher between his shoulder blades determined to make him submit.

He groaned softly and let out a pained sigh, his voice becoming more pleading. "Little one... come on... just let me go." His tone took on a slightly desperate quality. "I'm your alpha... you can't do this to me." He tried to push himself up off the ground again, continuing to struggle against my weight.

I smirked burying my nose in the nape of his neck.

He inhaled sharply, his body trembling slightly, his voice becoming more desperate and pleading as he spoke. "Luna.... please. I can't submit to you like this. I don't want to have to hurt you."

I giggled. "What happened to not holding back?"

He sighed softly. "You know if I wasn't holding back right now… you wouldn't be able to hold me down like this."

I leaned down, my mouth just an inch from his ear. "Then. Don't. Hold. Back."

He let out an annoyed growl and shook his head slowly, his voice becoming more irritated. "You don't know what you're asking for. I'm going to break your hold on me... and once I do... Are you really sure about this?"

I lowered my face against his, and a low growl escaped me. "Your precious luna found her power. You keep holding back, you won't see my full potential."

He inhaled sharply, his body trembling slightly as my low growl sent chills down his spine, his voice becoming more excited. "You have no idea what you're asking for." His voice took on a slightly desperate quality. "I don't want to hurt you... I could seriously injure you if I do this. Do you still want me to break your hold on me?"

I gave a short nod and bared my teeth. "Show me the alpha in you or I'll never submit." He let out a deep growl and squeezed his eyes shut, struggling against my hold on him for a moment before finally breaking free and pushing me off him.

He stood up straight and looked down at me, his voice becoming more determined. "Fine... you asked for it. Let's see if you can handle my full power." He smirked and started circling me, keeping an eye on my every move.

I continued to channel his strength, the rush of his power coursing through me like a fire ignited in my veins. I kept my eyes on him waiting for his next move. I growled as I stood up as well and bared my teeth once more. "Try me."

He let out a deep growl and lunged toward me, his body moving with incredible speed and agility. He moved in close and wrapped one arm around my waist while using the other to deliver a powerful blow to my ribs, trying to throw me off balance. "Let's see what you've got, luna...don't disappoint me."

I winced as the hit landed, my ribs now throbbing. I quickly regained my composure. Time for another trick Ryker and Shade taught me.

I sank my teeth into his arm, focusing on my wolf but just enough for my teeth to take shape, clamping down harder on his arm.

He groaned softly and grimaced in pain. "You can't use your wolf against me like this." He tried to pull away but my teeth were firmly embedded in his arm, causing him to growl softly in frustration.

I finally let go, not giving him a second to breathe before I attacked again. "You should know I'll take any advantage I can."

He let out a low growl as my teeth sunk back into his arm, my speed and agility catching him off guard. His body trembled slightly as he struggled to stay on his feet. "You really don't know what you're asking for, do you? You're not just fighting me, luna... you're fighting your own wolf." He tried to pull away again but I was relentless in my attacks. I won't lie, the rush was overwhelming but I was anchored enough to avoid shifting fully.

I pulled away and backed off of him wiping his blood from my mouth. "I concede."

He let out a deep breath, his body trembling slightly as he slowly regained control of himself. "Luna... you are something else." He paused for a moment, trying to remain calm despite the excitement in his voice. "You know... that was really impressive, luna... I'm impressed. You're growing up quickly... I'm proud of you, luna."

I blushed and looked down to the ground. "I've had great teachers."

He smiled softly and looked down at me. "Luna... don't be so modest. You may have had great teachers… but you also have a strong will and determination." He chuckled softly and shook his head. "You didn't learn that from anyone else, luna… that's all you."

I sighed and lay down in the grass beneath me. I could still taste his blood on my teeth and it was invigorating.

He chuckled softly and knelt beside me, looking down at me as he spoke. "You know… I never thought I would see the day when my luna would be able to take me down." He smirked and shook his head, his voice becoming more amused as he spoke. "If you keep this up… you might just make me proud. But don't get too cocky, luna... you still have a long way to go before you can beat me."

I smiled and sighed. "You're right."

He smiled softly and lay down next to me, looking up at the stars. "I've always known you had what it takes, luna… but you've really outdone yourself today. I'm so proud of you, luna... I know your parents would be too." He chuckled softly and turned to look at me, his eyes sparkling with admiration. "But if they saw how much blood you just tasted... they might not be quite so proud anymore."

I rolled onto my side to face him. "Why do you keep calling me by my title?" I looked at him intently.

He shrugged and smiled softly, his voice becoming more playful. "Why not? It's who you are. You're the luna of this pack... it suits you." He chuckled softly and turned to look at me, his eyes sparkling with amusement. "Besides... it's fun seeing how flustered it makes you."

I shook my head with a shy smile. "I like it better when you call me little one."

He smirked and chuckled softly. "And what makes you think I'm going to call you that? Little luna... that's your new nickname from now on." He grinned and shook his head, his tone taking on a slightly challenging quality. "If you want me to call you by your real name again... then you're just going to have to earn it."

I smiled shyly at him, my eyes meeting his. "I missed this…"

He smiled back at me, his voice becoming gentler and more tender as he spoke. "I missed it too, luna. It's been so long since we've just been able to lay here together... enjoying each other's company." He looked up at the stars as he continued to speak. "I've missed this more than you know, luna."

I sighed as I leaned my head on his chest. "I'm sorry I didn't stay to watch the stars with you. I was too mad at you."

He smiled softly and wrapped his arm around me, pulling me closer to him as he spoke. "luna... you don't need to apologize. I shouldn't have left you like that... I was just so worried about the pack that I forgot what was really important." He sighed softly and looked down at me, his eyes sparkling with affection. "You're my mate, luna... you should always be my first priority."

I smiled softly as I looked up at the stars, my hand resting on his chest. "I'm sorry for being a brat."

He chuckled softly and looked down at me. "You're not being a brat right now, luna... you're just being yourself." He smiled and shook his head, his tone taking on a slightly playful quality. "And I love every part of you... even the bratty parts." His eyes sparkled with amusement as he looked down at me.

I smiled as I looked up at the stars, feeling like I could stay there forever.

"Luna, can I ask you something?"

I smiled softly and looked up at him, my eyes meeting his. "You can ask me anything, Grey."

He smiled softly and paused for a moment, trying to gather the courage to ask what he really wanted to ask me. "Luna... do you remember when I left that night?"

I nodded softly, remembering the pain I felt that night.

He sighed softly and looked down at me, his voice becoming more sincere. "I need you to know that I didn't leave because of you." He paused for a moment and took a deep breath, trying to remain calm despite the pain in his voice. "That night... I was just so overwhelmed by everything... the pack... my duties as alpha, your teasing." He sighed softly again and shook his head, his tone taking on a slightly frustrated quality. "I'm sorry, luna... I never wanted to hurt you like that."

I looked up at him. "I wish you had stayed."

He paused for a moment and looked down at me, his voice becoming gentler and more tender as he spoke. "I wish I had too." His eyes sparkled with compassion as he looked down at me. He tried to hold back his own tears. "If I could go back in time and change things... I would." He smiled softly and stroked my hair gently, trying to comfort me. "But I can't go back in time, all we have is right now."

I leaned into him, not able to find my words. I just didn't want to think about that night anymore.

He sighed softly and pulled me closer to him, his voice becoming more soothing as he spoke. "It's alright... we don't have to talk about it anymore. Let's just enjoy each other's company... forget about everything else for tonight." He smiled softly and stroked my hair gently, continuing to comfort me. His eyes sparkled with affection as he looked down at me, his voice taking on a slightly pleading quality. "Please don't be sad, luna."

I nodded weakly, taking a deep breath.

I snuggled further into his embrace. He continued to stroke my hair. "I can tell you want to ask me something. Is there something on your mind?"

"I want to come home..." I couldn't bring myself to look up at home in fear of what he'd say.

He sighed softly. "Luna... you can come home anytime you want. But... are you sure that's what you really want? You left for a reason... do you really think coming back is what's best for you?"

I sat up and looked at him. "If there's anything I've learned in getting to know the pack in the past two weeks... The mate bond is... it isn't something I can run from... What happened between us hurt like hell but it's time we move forward." I smiled despite the pain weighing in my heart.

He smiled softly and looked at me, becoming more sincere. "Luna... I'm so proud of you." He paused for a moment, a hint of pride in his voice. "You're right, luna... the mate bond is something we can't escape." He chuckled softly and shook his head, his tone taking on a slightly playful quality. "Besides... if I could live with you again after what happened between us, then nothing can ever separate us again."

I giggled. "I'll hold you to that."

He smiled softly and stroked my hair gently. "I'm glad you decided to come home, luna. You really don't know how much this means to me.... How happy I am to have you back." His eyes sparkled with affection. "I don't want to be alone anymore."

I took his hand in mine as I leaned into his touch. "A thousand hunters couldn't keep me away."

He wrapped his arm around me, pulling me closer to him. "Luna... you really do know how to make a man feel special. But there's no need to flatter me, I'm just glad to have you back home again." He smiled gently and brushed a strand of hair out of my eyes.

I leaned into his touch. He was the only one who could make me feel this way.

He smiled softly and pulled away from me. "I never thought I'd see this day, you know? You running into my arms willingly, telling me how much you missed me..." He chuckled softly and shook his head. "But it feels so good to hear those words from your lips." His eyes looked between my eyes and my lips.

I knew he wanted to kiss me. I felt my skin start to heat up under his gaze almost as if on cue. I knew I was going into heat again. My skin felt like it was on fire and I wanted nothing more than to rip his clothes off.

He seemed to notice the heat beneath my skin. "Luna... you're feeling it again, aren't you?" He paused for a moment and took a deep breath, trying to remain calm despite the concern in his voice. "Your heat... do you think we should take this somewhere else?" His eyes sparkled with amusement as he looked at me, trying to keep from laughing at the look on my face.

I took a deep breath and nodded. His scent lingered in the air driving me into a trance.

He chuckled softly and stood up. "Let's go, luna... before you lose control of yourself." He offered me his hand and looked down at me with a smirk on his face, the excitement in his eyes betraying how much he wanted to watch me lose control of myself. "You might regret it later if you don't let me help you with this."

I took his hand. My body felt a bit wobbly as his scent overwhelmed my senses. My skin ignited in temperature. He smiled softly and started walking with me. "Your heat is kicking in already, luna. I can practically hear your wolf trying to break free. You're going to be a handful tonight... but I can't wait to see you lose yourself in pleasure." His eyes sparkled with amusement.

I started to feel overwhelmed by the heat. "I need you..."

He stopped walking, his voice becoming more confident and commanding as he spoke. "I know you do. I can feel it too. Let's hurry up... I don't want to keep you waiting any longer than necessary." He smirked and started walking again, faster this time, leading me towards the pack house.

Chapter Twelve

It felt like an eternity to get to the pack house, fighting every urge to stop and take what my body craved. We made it to his bedroom. I was starting to burn up even more. He opened the door to his bedroom, his voice becoming more confident and commanding as he spoke.

"Come on, luna... we can't wait any longer." He smiled softly and pulled me into the room, closing the door behind him. "You're mine... I'm going to take you now and there's nothing you can do about it." His eyes sparkled with excitement as he looked down at me, his voice taking on a slightly seductive quality. "I want to hear you scream my name as you lose control of yourself... so let go, luna... give in to me."

I had lost all sense of control, my body burning up with an intense heat. He smirked and pulled me closer to him, his voice becoming more confident and commanding as he spoke. "Let it all go... I want you to let your wolf take over. You're going to feel so much better once you let yourself go." He leaned down and whispered in my ear, "I want to hear your wolf howl for me... don't hold back."

That was all I needed to hear.

I let out a low growl and pulled him against me by the collar of his button-up, kissing him hungrily as I guided him over to the bed. He grinned and pushed me down onto the bed. "That's it... give in to your instincts. I want you to lose control of yourself... I want to feel every part of your wolf... every moan and growl you make. Let me hear you scream my name."

I quickly scrambled on the bed to my knees, a growl escaping me as my fingers tore through the buttons of his shirt. I pulled him down on top of me, kissing him so desperately it was hard to control my breathing. I wrapped my legs around his waist as my fingers tangled in his hair.

I broke the kiss for a moment. "Enough talking." My lips crashed against his once more.

He grinned and wrapped his arms around me, pulling me closer to him. "I agree... we've talked enough for tonight."

He kissed me softly and started kissing his way down my neck, trying to tease me a little before he gave in to our needs. I moaned softly as his lips touched my neck, my body responding to his touch.

He kissed my neck again, his voice becoming more confident and seductive as he spoke. "You're so sensitive, luna... it drives me crazy." He chuckled softly and kissed my neck again, trying to tease me a little more. "You taste so good, Luna... I want to taste every inch of your body tonight."

I gasped as he flipped me over onto my stomach. His hands gripped my tights at the seam and tore them open until he could remove them completely.

He grinned and pushed me down onto the bed. "Let me help you with those, luna... I don't want you to waste any time. You're so beautiful, Naphinae... I want to worship every part of your body tonight." His eyes sparkled with desire as he looked down at me. "Let me make you feel good, luna... let me make up for all that time we were apart."

I gasped as he positioned himself on top of me, his weight on my back. He pressed himself against me. "You feel so good. I've missed this. I want to give you everything you need." His eyes sparkled with desire as he looked down at me. "But first... I think it's time for some payback."

I gasped again as he took hold of my wrists, pinning them behind my back. He pressed himself against me again, his voice becoming more confident. "Payback's a bitch... you're going to learn that tonight. Let me make you feel how I felt when you left me... I want to show you what it was like to be abandoned." He smiled softly and kissed the back of my neck.

I bit my lip and propped myself up on my knees, pushing my ass up against his already hard length. The only thing separating us from feeling one another, my dark green panties and his dark gray suit pants. He grinned and started kissing my neck again, his voice becoming more confident and seductive as he spoke. "You're so beautiful, luna... I love how you look when you beg for me, when you're desperate for me." His eyes sparkled with desire as he looked down at me, his voice taking on a slightly teasing quality. "But I'm not going to let you have it just yet... I want to make you suffer first." He chuckled softly and pulled away from my neck for a moment. "Beg for me, luna. I want to hear how much you need me."

I bit my lip and groaned softly, desperate for his touch. "G-Grey..."

He looked down at me, his eyes darkening with desire. "Beg for me, luna... I want to hear how much you need this... tell me what you really want."

I moaned deeply, unable to resist the urge to grind against him. He pushed me back onto the bed.

"That's good, luna... I knew you wouldn't be able to resist for long. I'm not going to give you what you want yet... I want you to beg a little more."

I moaned deeply, my voice becoming breathier and pleading. "Please, Grey..."

He pulled away from me again. "Please what, luna? You need to ask for what you want if you want me to give it to you. So ask me again..." The amount of heat my body was building was becoming unbearable.

My voice becoming breathier and more desperate, I moaned deeply. "Please, Grey, I need you."

He climbed on top of me. "That's better... I love it when you beg for me. Now tell me what you really want, luna... be specific." He pressed himself against me again.

I gasped softly, feeling the weight of his body on mine. He held himself against me.

"I know you want me, luna... I can feel it." He paused for a moment and took a deep breath. "You're mine Naphinae Kent... I own your body now. So show me how much you need me... show me how much you belong to me."

My head snapped up as I felt his fingers push my panties to the side, moaning as his fingers teased me from my clit up. "Grey, please… I can't take it. I need you." The fire beneath my skin continued to increase in intensity.

He pushed me back onto the bed. "You're so needy, Luna... I love it when you beg for me. But if you want my touch, then you have to give me something in return." He chuckled softly and pulled away from me, moving towards his dresser. "What do you think I want from you?" He glanced at me from over his shoulder with a smirk on his face.

I rolled onto my back, my breathing getting heavier. I looked over at him and curiosity peaked despite how hot I was getting. "What?"

He pulled out a pair of handcuffs from his dresser drawer. "Do you see these handcuffs?" He held them up in front of me and smiled mischievously. "I want you to put these on for me... That's an order, luna... that is if you want what I have to offer."

I hesitated for a moment, feeling both intrigued and nervous about the prospect.

He smiled and moved towards the bed. "Don't be scared, luna... I promise this will be fun. Just put them on... I want to see how good you look when you're bound and at my mercy." His eyes sparkled with deep desire as he looked down at me. "And don't worry... if you don't like it, you can take them off whenever you want."

I held out my wrists, hesitant but excited to try something new. "I trust you Grey."

He smiled softly and put the handcuffs on my wrists, making sure they were tight enough to keep me in place but not too tight. "There, that's a good girl." He sat back and looked down at me. "Now lie down. I want you to stay right there while I take what I want from you. And trust me... you're going to enjoy this as much as I am."

I obediently lay down on the bed, his dominating presence making my heart race.

He moved towards the bed. "You look so beautiful like that, luna... so vulnerable and helpless." His eyes scanned over me, taking in the sight of me bound. "And now I'm going to take what I want from you... but you're not allowed to move from this position. Do you understand me, luna?"

I nod, my voice trembling a bit. "I understand...."

He smiled and climbed on top of me again. "Good girl... you're doing so well already. Now let's see if I can make you scream my name..." His eyes sparkled with desire as he looked down at me. "Let's see if I can make you beg for more."

I moaned, the fire beneath my skin increasing in intensity. "Greyson... it's... starting to hurt..."

He chuckled softly. "That's the point... I want you to suffer. But it doesn't have to hurt if you just give into your wolf... let go of everything except for me." He started to take off his shirt, revealing the tattoos covering his muscular torso. "Let me make you feel good... let me take away all your pain and replace it with pleasure."

I screamed in agony, tears streaming down my face as my heat cycle intensified. "Grey... it's too much..."

He grinned. "Just relax, luna... let yourself go. It'll be alright... I promise." He started to kiss my neck again, this time biting me softly.

I gasped softly, tilting my head back as his hand slipped under my panties. His fingers rubbing circles around my clit, causing moans to escape me. He smirked and started to unbutton his pants. "That's it... Let me make you feel good... let me give you everything you need."

I moaned loudly, the fire beneath my skin increasing in intensity. "Greyson... please..." My breathing became more ragged as I was overwhelmed by desire.

He started to take off his pants, revealing his muscular body underneath. "That's good, luna... that's exactly what I want to hear. Just relax and let me take care of you... that's all I want to do."

I watched as he took off his boxers then climbed back on the bed. The heat coursing through me with the intensity of the sun. He moved toward me. "I can see how much you want this, luna... how much you need it. Do you want me to give it to you? Do you want me to take away all your pain and give you something even better?"

I bit my lip, attempting to suppress a scream. My body heat intensified beyond what I'd experienced the first time. "Grey... please!"

As he touched my skin, I was burning up beyond what I should in heat. I was scared and in pain, this felt like he was treating this like a game. "I'm sorry I left you Grey… please… I can't take it anymore…" I was panting heavily and as the heat radiated through me, discomfort lead straight to pain.

I felt tears roll down the sides of my face, the pain I was in was unbearable. "Make it stop!" I was starting to become desperate. I could see his resolve to be dominant slip, his concern for my well-being starting to show. My tears fell faster and I shut my eyes tightly. I started to feel dizzy like I would pass out at any moment.

He paused for a moment. "Luna… are you ok?" He sounded worried and concerned. "Are you feeling alright?" He moved closer to me, his voice taking on a slightly gentle quality. "Is the pain too much? Please tell me what I can do to help you feel better."

I clenched my teeth, trying to hold back the pain. "I-I just want it to stop." Tears streamed down my face as I looked at him.

He removed the handcuffs and picked me up. I clung to him desperately as he carried me to the shower. He turned on the water as cold as he could get it, but my body temperature was so high that the cold water hitting my skin sent a thick steam through the bathroom. He sighed softly and wrapped his arms around me, trying to keep me close while also making sure I didn't fall. "I know it's cold… but I promise this will help you feel better. Just relax…let me try to cool your body down a little bit." He started to kiss my neck again, trying to distract me from the cold water hitting my skin. I held onto him tightly, sobbing uncontrollably as the cold water hit my hot skin.

I started to feel faint, my vision was starting to blur. My grip on him weakened. He picked me up and spread my legs, pinning me against the wall of the shower. The cold tiling of the wall hitting my skin burned but I was so out of it, I couldn't feel it.

He grunted as he pinned me against the wall, trying to keep me still as he continued to kiss my neck. His voice became more desperate as he spoke. "Don't you dare lose consciousness, luna… not yet." His voice took on a slightly pleading quality. "I know it hurts right now, but please just hold on a little longer." He continued to kiss my neck and hold me close.

I could feel him pushing himself into me, adjusting to how tight I was compared to his size. I was so disoriented that I couldn't react. He grunted as pushed himself deeper inside of me, his voice becoming more desperate as he spoke. "Luna... don't let me lose you like this." He took a deep breath, trying to remain calm despite the urgency in his voice. "Please... I need you to hold on for just a little while longer." As he continued to push himself into me, I was losing consciousness from the pain and the cold.

He continued to push himself deeper. "Please, Luna... don't give up on me now. I need you... I need you so much," he spoke through gritted teeth, his concern outweighing his pleasure although it was still hinted in his tone.

His movements became faster and more erratic, causing a cry of pain to escape from my lips. He grunted as he started to move faster, his voice becoming more desperate as he spoke. "Naphinae... I'm so close, I just need you to hold on for a little longer. Please don't let this be our last time together... I need you to trust me." He continued to hold me close. I felt him bite down on my shoulder sending a shock through my system and snapping me back to reality. I gasped as his teeth sunk into my shoulder, breaking through my skin with ease.

The cold water washed away the blood dripping down. I whimpered from the symphony of overwhelming sensations. His teeth sunk deeper into my shoulder, his voice becoming more desperate as he spoke. "Just hold on a little bit longer." His eyes sparkled with concern as he looked at me. "Please don't let go... I need you." He looked down at my shoulder and saw the blood running down it, and his expression became one of concern and regret.

My head tilted back, a combination of whimpers and moans taking turns escaping me. I was enjoying this but it hurt. My tears continued to fall as my body surrendered, trusting him with every ounce of strength I had left. He sighed softly and pulled away, his voice becoming more compassionate as he spoke. "Naphinae... I'm so sorry."

He took a moment trying to remain calm, concern taking over in his voice. "I never meant to hurt you, not like this." He looked down at my shoulder, seeing the blood running down it, and his expression became one of worry. "I'll take care of this... just let me help you feel better first." He kissed my neck again, trying to distract me from the pain while also cleaning up the wound on my shoulder.

I whimpered softly, my body still shaking from the intense pleasure. "It's alright, Grey."

He sighed softly, his voice becoming gentle. "No it's not... I never meant to hurt you... I'll take care of this... just let me help you feel better first." He started to clean up the wound on my shoulder with some water from the shower, using his other hand to hold me close.

I moaned softly as he continued his rhythmic movements, slowly and lovingly. I felt my pleasure building and the heat beginning to subside as he took care of my shoulder. He smiled softly at me and continued to clean up my shoulder. "There, all better." He looked down at my shoulder, seeing the blood had finally stopped running down, and his expression became one of relief. "Are you feeling better now? I never meant to hurt you... I just wanted to make you feel good but instead, I was caught up in what I wanted." He held me close while continuing his movements, trying to distract me from any lingering discomfort.

I moaned softly as his movements began to pick up in pace. "Grey..."

He held me tighter as his thrusting began to consume him. The sounds of our hips meeting echoing through the bathroom.

He grunted softly and continued to move, his voice becoming more passionate. "Luna... I never knew how much I needed this. Just tell me what you need and I'll do it... I'm here for you." He looked down at my shoulder again, the wound almost fully healed, and his expression became one of relief. "You have no idea how much you mean to me, luna..."

I moaned softly, feeling his movements quicken. I held on to him tightly, my body starting to enjoy the moment. I gasped and held on a little tighter, my nails digging into his shoulders for support as he pushed himself deeper into me.

He grunted and continued to move against me. "I'm not going to last much longer. Luna…" He looked down at my shoulder. The wound was completely healed. "You have no idea how much you mean to me…"

I leaned my head against his shoulder allowing myself to surrender completely to him, the heat in my body fading. "Don't stop… please…" I started to feel overwhelmed, my mind a complete mess and I was unable to sift through it.

He grunted as he picked up his pace, his voice was more desperate. "Luna… I'm almost there." His voice took on a slightly pleading quality. "Just let me give this to you… just let me make you feel good."

My stomach began to knot up and my body tensed. I could feel him so much more as I tightened around him. Whimpers escaped me at a consistent rate. I held on to him tighter, my nails digging into his shoulders further.

He continued to move, his voice becoming even more desperate as he spoke. "I'm there, just hold on a little longer." He paused for a moment grunting deeply, trying to remain calm despite the sensations he was feeling. His eyes were filled with lust and desire as he looked down at me with a shy smile. "Please… I need this… I need you to feel good." He tucked his hand under my chin, lifting my head, and kissed me as he held me close.

I returned his kiss, pouring every emotion I felt into it. I could feel myself tightening around him further, my body slowly beginning to tremble in his arms. I broke the kiss and my head fell back against the wall. "Fuck!" My whimpers turned into moans, filling the air with an intoxicating desire. My body begged for release.

He started to move more forcefully, his voice becoming even more desperate as he spoke. "I can't hold back any longer."

I picked my head up, biting my lip as I saw how hard he was fighting against himself. "Let go Greyson. I'm right here."

He looked at me, his eyes full of desire. "I don't want to hurt you." His voice was filled with concern, his expression becoming one of worry. "Are you sure?"

I moved my hands from his shoulders, bringing one to cup his face and the other running through his hair as I looked him in the eye. "Let go Grey. It's what you need and what I want."

He looked back at me and saw my pleading eyes, his expression becoming one of determination. He sighed softly and let go, his voice becoming desperate. "Luna… please forgive me if I hurt you." He grunted as he started to move again, his voice taking on a pleading quality. "I'm sorry… it's just so hard to hold back." He leaned in closer to me and started to kiss my neck again, trying to distract us both from the overwhelming sensations we were feeling build.

My moans increased in volume, I couldn't hold myself back anymore either. "Greyson… I… I can't…" My moans cut me off as I unraveled completely.

My orgasm tore through me relentlessly as his pace increased. I could feel him tensing up, he was right behind me allowing himself the satisfaction of his own release. I wrapped my arms around him, holding him tightly as we both panted, enjoying the moment we had just shared.

He sighed softly and started to slow his movements. His voice was softer as he spoke. "That was amazing."

He held me close and pressed himself against me, enjoying the warmth of my body and the feeling of being so close to each other.

Chapter Thirteen

Once my body temperature returned to normal, he warmed the water to the shower and we helped each other clean up. After we finished showering, Greyson carried me to bed and helped me get dressed before he dressed himself.

"Thank you." I was sincere, I appreciated his care. We lay down in bed and I snuggled against his chest, my head resting just above his heart.

He kissed my forehead and smiled softly. "You're welcome, luna. I'm just happy that you feel better now." He pulled me closer and held me tightly against him, enjoying the warmth of our bodies being so close.

"Grey, can I ask you something?" I looked up at him, genuinely curious. He looked down at me with a soft smile. "Of course. What's on your mind?" I looked down, My fingers tracing the tattoos on his chest. "I know that heat is when my body my body tells me I need you, but why does that happen to me? Why is it so intense?"

He chuckled softly. "It's because you're a werewolf, luna. Your body is reacting to mine because you feel safe with me... you trust me. The heat tells you that I'm yours... and that you're mine."

I nodded, still not looking up at him. "I get that... but what exactly is heat?" I started to feel a bit flustered.

His voice was gentle as he spoke. "Heat is a form of desire, luna. It's when your body craves someone... and it makes you feel hot... warm... and tingly." He chuckled softly and rubbed his hand over my shoulder. "It also means you want someone to take care of you... and that's exactly what I want to do for you."

I continued tracing the patterns of his tattoos. "I don't know, it just feels like there's more to it. If there's anything I've learned about being a wolf since I've been here… Everything has a deeper meaning, a deeper value." I finally looked up at him.

He looked down at me and smiled softly. "You're right, luna. Everything does have a deeper meaning... including heat. The heat isn't just about attraction or desire... it's about wanting to be with someone on a deeper level." He paused for a moment, trying to find the right words. "It's when you feel safe enough with someone to let go of your inhibitions... and it's when you know you can trust them with everything... even your most intimate thoughts and desires."

I look into his eyes, feeling my heart skip a beat. "Grey…" I trailed off, unsure of how to express what I was feeling.

He smiled softly, his voice became even more gentle as he spoke. "Yes? What's on your mind?" He rubbed his hand over my shoulder again, enjoying the warmth of my body.

I sat up and turned to look at him. "My family weren't really there for me… Never being able to shift, I was seen as an abomination. Nothing of value as far as bonds or anything pack related, nothing was ever explained to me." I sighed, and looked down at my hands. "I want to be the mate you deserve but… I can't help but feel so uneducated toward so many different topics as far as everything goes."

He smiled softly and pulled me back down to the bed. "Naphinae... you're already the perfect mate for me. Just having you in my life is enough for me... I don't need anything else." He kissed my forehead and rubbed his hand over my shoulder, enjoying being close to me.

I looked up at him and smiled softly. "Grey, you really mean it?" I asked, looking up at him with a grateful expression.

He nodded as he smiled softly. "Of course. I don't need anything else from you Naphinae... just knowing you're by my side is enough." He pauses for a moment and brought his hand up to cup my face, making sure I was looking at him. "I love you, Naphinae... more than anything in the world." He leaned in closer and kissed me tenderly. Joy flooded through me as he confessed his love. I wrapped my arms around him tightly and hugged him close. He wrapped his arms around me and hugged me tightly. "I love you, my luna... I love you so much." He smiled softly as he pulled me into another kiss.

He pulled away from the kiss for a moment and looked at me, his voice taking on a slightly pleading quality. "Luna... could you do me a favor?"

I felt a pang of panic strike my chest. "Is something wrong?" I furrowed my eyebrows in concern of what he'd say.

He shook his head and smiled softly, it was reassuring. "No... it's nothing like that. I just... I want to ask if you would... be willing to shift into your wolf form with me?" He looked at me with a soft smile. He looked like a child begging their mom for candy or a new toy.

I giggled, a shy smile tugging at the corners of my lips. "You don't think it's a bit late? I mean the sun should be coming up soon."

He chuckled softly and shook his head. "No, luna... I don't think it's too late." He looked at me again. "I just want to spend some time with you in your wolf form... away from everyone else. Please? It would mean a lot to me." He nuzzled his face into my hair, holding me a little tighter.

I sighed playfully and nodded slowly. "I guess, we could shift for a little while." I spoke with slight hesitation, but I was willing to do this for him.

He kissed my cheek. "Thank you, luna... I really appreciate it. I've been wanting to spend some time with you in your wolf form for a while now... I just wanted to make sure you were comfortable first." He kissed my cheek again and held me tighter. My cheeks turned a deep shade of red and I turned away, a shy smile tugging at the corners of my lips. He gently cupped my face, turning my head to look at him again. "Don't be so shy, you don't have to hide your face from me... not anymore." I leaned up against him and tangled my fingers in his hair, bringing him closer to me and pulling him into a loving kiss.

He leaned into the kiss and wrapped his arms around me, pulling me even closer to him. He kissed me back with passion and desire. "Luna... I love you so much." He pulled away from the kiss for a moment and looked down at me as he brushed a lock of hair behind my ear. "Please... don't ever doubt how much I love you." He pulled me back into another deep and tender kiss. I smiled softly and blushed, my cheeks turned a deeper shade of red.

He chuckled softly and rubbed his hand over my shoulder. "Come on... it's time for us to shift." He smiled softly again and kissed my cheek. "I want to see you in your wolf form... I want to see you the way you really are."

I looked up at him with a shy smile. "Let's at least get outside first."

He smiled with a small nod. "Of course, luna." He lifted me up and carried me outside, setting me down on the ground in front of a large clearing in the woods. He took a deep breath and looked up at the sky. "Are you ready, luna?" He turned to look at me.

I nodded slowly, looking up at the sky and taking a deep breath, my voice filled with uncertainty. "I'm ready, Grey." I started to shift, feeling the fur and muscles form on my body, my bones breaking and realigning as I transformed into my wolf form.

I stood on all fours and howled into the slow-shifting night sky. He stared in awe as I transformed before his eyes. The shift didn't hurt nearly as much as it did the first few times, I have Shade and Ryker to thank for that. He took a deep breath to ready himself and shifted his body into its wolf form. The breaking of his bones didn't seem to phase him. He looked up at the sky with a sense of wonder and awe. He howled back at me.

He ran around in circles, enjoying the freedom of not having to worry about anything else. He looked up at the night sky again, taking it all in. I've never truly gotten to see his wolf form, it was truly a sight to behold. His coat was pure black with a few white patches through his fur, his eyes were a deep red that glowed slightly.

We spent the hours of dawn chasing each other through the woods. He showed me parts of our territory that I hadn't gotten to explore. The beauty of the land we hold was untouched. After a while, I couldn't keep up and decided I'd shift back once we reached the lake.

I sat at the edge of the water and took in the sight of the sunrise reflecting against the water as I attempted to catch my breath after shifting back.

He shifted back into his human form and walked over, sitting down next to me at the edge of the water. He looked around, enjoying the beauty of the land we hold. He turned his head and smiled at me before returning his gaze up to the sky. "It's so peaceful here... I don't think there's anything better than watching a sunrise or sunset on our territory." He reached over and put his arm around my shoulder.

I looked down at my hands. I had a bad feeling sinking in. He looked down at me and noticed the look of concern on his face. "Luna? Are you okay?" He rubbed my shoulder again and smiled softly. "What's wrong, love?" He leaned in closer and kissed my cheek.

I looked up at him and brushed a lock of my hair away from my face and behind my ear before looking back down at my hands. "I'm not sure." I looked back up at him, biting my lip nervously. "The past 16 hours have been amazing. I am happy to be back by your side... I guess I just feel like something is going to happen."

He looked at me and took my hands in his, trying to reassure me. "Luna, everything is going to be alright. The past 16 hours have been amazing... just being with you again makes me so happy. I don't care what happens next... as long as I'm with you, that's all that matters." He kissed my cheek again and rubbed his hand over my shoulder.

I sighed, shaking my head and looking down at the ground. "I just feel like something bad is going to happen." I looked back up at him, my eyes filled with worry.

"Luna, I promise... nothing bad is going to happen. I love you more than anything in this world... and I'll do everything in my power to protect you." He held me tighter against him, continuing to rub my shoulder. I sighed, pulling away slightly. He looked at me with concern and paused for a moment to try to remain calm. "Luna?" He reached out and took my hands in his again. "Is something wrong?" He looked down at our hands and kissed the top of my hand gently.

I stared off into the distance, a worried look on my face. He looked at me with concern and took a moment, taking a deep breath to try to remain calm. "Luna?" He reached out and turned my face towards him. "Is something wrong?" He rubbed his hand over my cheek, trying to offer me a bit of reassurance. "Please... talk to me." His voice took on a slightly pleading quality as he spoke. He looked into my eyes and smiled softly again.

I sighed and plastered a fake smile on my face to offer him some comfort. "Let's just enjoy this before having to go back to the pack house." I held my hand over his and rubbed his hand with my thumb.

Chapter Fourteen

We got back to the pack house a couple of hours after the sun came up. We both showered and got dressed. Today would be my first official day as luna. As we were getting dressed for the day I turned to Greyson as I finished putting on my heels.

"Hey, Grey?"

He looked up from putting on his jacket and smiled at me.

"Yes, Luna?"

He raised an eyebrow and waited for me to continue.

"I realize Shade doesn't have an official title… Do you think we could make her an official Beta?" I smiled shyly and furrowed my eyebrows, hoping he'd agree.

He chuckled softly and shook his head, his voice taking on a slightly playful quality as he spoke. "No, luna… you know that would never happen. Shade doesn't want an official title… she's happy just being your second-in-command." He reached out and touched my arm. "She doesn't need any formal recognition… she already knows how important she is to you."

I looked up at him as he approached me. "I really feel she deserves it. She takes care of everyone, no matter how old. She's valuable to the pack."

He smiled softly and wrapped his arms around me, pulling me close to him. "Luna… I know how important she is to you… and you're right, she takes care of everyone no matter how old, but we both know that Shade doesn't want an official title…" He looked down at me and kissed my cheek.

I sighed heavily, feeling defeated. "I understand. I just really wish she had that title." He rubbed my arm. "I know, luna… I know." He sighed, feeling just as defeated himself. "But sometimes, we have to accept that someone else doesn't want the same things that we do. Shade has already done so much for you... she doesn't need an official title to show how important she is to you."

I nodded slowly, realizing he was right. "I know she doesn't need an official title." I took a deep breath and looked up at him. "But she's still valuable to the pack, and I want to acknowledge that."

He smiled softly and nodded. "You're right. She is valuable to the pack, and you already do acknowledge that... you always treat her with respect and you always value her opinion." He kissed my cheek again, rubbing his hand over my shoulder.

I thought on it for a moment. "Okay... No official title, but... What if we honored her in some way?" I looked up at him hopeful.

He looked down at me with a sense of curiosity in his eyes, intrigue in his voice. "What did you have in mind, luna? We could honor her in some way...... but what would be the best way to do that?"

I smiled at him. "Well, we could have a gathering and honor her in front of the whole pack. We could have her speak and share her wisdom and experience."

His eyes stood locked with mine as his smile widened. He nodded his head and his hands rubbed my shoulders, gently massaging them. "That's an interesting idea... We could definitely host a gathering in Shade's honor, but we can't force her into speaking. We don't know if she'll be comfortable with that."

I placed my hand over his and kept my eyes on his. "I'll talk to her when I find time today. What's on the list of things to do today?"

He smiled down at me softly, his voice becoming even more gentle as he spoke. "Well, we have a few things that need to be taken care of today. We need to go over the schedule for the next couple of weeks... We also need to have another meeting with the leaders of the neighboring packs... and we also need to make sure all of our territory is secure."

I nodded as I listened to what he was saying, taking mental notes. "Okay, so what's first, and where can I help?"

He kept his eyes on mine with a soft smile. "Let's start with the schedule for the next couple of weeks... we can go over that first. Once we go over the schedule, we can move on to meeting with the leaders of the neighboring packs... and then we'll end our day by making sure all of our territory is secure." He hugged me close, rubbing my back.

I nodded and took a deep breath. "I'll get the schedule ready, and you can go over it with me." I paused for a moment and looked up at him, feeling worried. "Will everything go as planned?"

He looked at me with a sense of concern, his voice taking on a slightly calming quality as he spoke. "Don't worry, luna... I'm sure everything will go as planned. We'll make sure that all of our plans are in place and that everyone knows what their role is in making them happen."

I nodded and took a deep breath. "Okay." I looked back up at him and smiled before giving him a quick kiss. "I'm ready when you are, alpha." I smirked.

He smiled softly and wrapped his arms around me, giving me a subtle squeeze. "Alright... let's go over the schedule for the next couple of weeks." He leaned in closer to me and kissed my cheek again. "I'll go over everything with you... and we'll make sure that all of our plans are in place."

I pulled away from him and grabbed my phone from the bed. I turned back to him feeling determined to make my first official day as luna go well. "Ready to get started when you are." I held out my hand to him.

He took my hand in his and squeezed it gently, his voice confident in quality as he spoke. "Let's do this." He led me out of the room and into his office, where he took a seat at the large wooden table in front of a wall filled with papers and documents. He looked over at me and smiled as he gestured for me to take a seat, his voice becoming even more gentle as he spoke. "Alright... let's go over everything." He takes a deep breath and pauses for a moment before beginning to go through all of the documents on the table.

We spent over an hour going through documents and making corrections as they were needed.

"Grey... If you weren't already a wolf I'd call you a dog. You really need to organize all these papers." I made myself chuckle, although that joke wasn't that funny.

He looked up from the documents he was working on and chuckled softly. "Alright... fair enough. I'll do my best to get this stuff organized... but it's been a busy few days."

I got up from where I was sitting and walked around the desk to sit on Greyson's lap. "If you get me the numbers for the other packs we have to meet with, I can start scheduling the meetings."

He smiled and wrapped his arms around me, pulling me close to him. "Sure... let me see if I can find those numbers." He looked up at me with a sense of tenderness, his voice soothing as he speaks. "Can I ask you something, luna?"

I leaned back against him and kissed his cheek. "Sure, what's on your mind?"

He looked down at me and smiled softly. "How do you feel about your first official day as luna? Are you happy with how things are going so far?" He rubbed his hand over my shoulders, releasing tension I hadn't realized was there.

I snuggled further into him. "I think we've barely scratched the surface of what needs to be done." I giggled and leaned my head against his shoulder. "I think you should go check the territory borders and I can stay here to make those phone calls." I looked over at him. "How's that sound?" I raised an eyebrow.

He looked at me with a sense of consideration. "That sounds like a good plan, luna... I'll go check the territory borders and you can make those phone calls, but don't take too long... we still need to get everything organized before the leaders from the neighboring packs arrive later today." He kissed my forehead.

I got up from sitting on his lap and took the papers with the numbers to the other packs that wouldn't be joining us for today. I waved at him as he left the room. "Be careful Grey."

He nodded, "Always little one." He closed the door, leaving me to the calls needing to be made.

The first call was nerve wracking, I should've asked Greyson how I should introduce myself. Every conversation got easier with the next call. By the end of it I had called at least five of our neighboring packs and set up meetings. I looked over the schedule and realized there was next to no free time for Greyson or myself.

I called for Shade and Tristan. I hoped this won't piss off Greyson. Between Shade, Tristan and myself, we coordinated a better schedule by shifting responsibilities. I made it clear that I expected reports about the tasks they were given after it was completed. Tristan left the room to go tend to Ashley, she was apparently expecting their first pup. As exciting as that was for them, it's Ashley so my excitement wasn't really there.

After Tristan left, it was just Shade and myself left. "Hey Shade, can you do me a favor and get me a list of the entirety of the pack? Names and ages please." She nodded and started to work on that for me. I finished finalizing the schedule while Shade worked on the list. After Shade handed me the list, I dismissed her to get ready for the meetings being held later.

When Greyson returned I was knee-deep in paperwork, I had piles of papers scattered across his desk. I was busy writing out a plan when he walked back into the office.

"Wow… You've been busy while I was gone. This is impressive luna. You've done a great job." He looked at me with a sense of admiration. "I can't believe you got all of this organized so quickly."

I peeled my eyes away from what I was doing and took in his appearance briefly, my eyes scanning across his clothes and skin. "No, no. Go shower before the other packs get here." I was stern but not enough to challenge his authority.

He looked down at himself and laughed as his eyes returned to mine. "Alright, alright. I'll go shower before the other pack leaders arrive." He paused for a moment, another laugh escaping him. "Don't worry luna, I won't be long." He smiled brightly and left the office again.

I dove back into what I was doing. I was making a plan for the younger wolves of the pack. Trying to sift through all the names and ages to make proper groupings.

In my time away from Greyson I noticed not many of the pack members ever train. I understand the youngest pups of the pack don't shift quite yet so I took that into account. I grouped the pack into age ranges from 13-15 and 16-19. I had hope that Ryker and Shade would work together on this but that isn't a guarantee. I also took it upon myself to set up a group for the youngest pups, ages 4-8 to go exploring with supervision of course.

When Greyson came back, I was just finishing up on some of the groupings but I was nowhere near done with finalizing. He came up behind me and wrapped his arms around my waist, hugging me and nuzzling into my hair. His scent lingering in the air was enough to catch my attention.

"Hi to you too." I giggled. I felt him smile against my neck before he kissed it.

"Hello, my luna. I missed you." He rocked us as he took enjoyment in holding me close to him. "How's everything coming along?"

I pulled away and turned to face him, rubbing my hands up and down his arms. "Why don't we sit and discuss everything?" He nodded and stepped around me, pulling out a chair for me to take a seat. "Thank you Grey." I smiled up at him. He smiled in return before taking his seat behind his desk.

"We've made some progress already, but there's still a lot left to be done." His eyebrows furrowed as he looked at me. "I know this is a lot to handle for your first day as Luna so…"

I nodded as I listened. "This is exactly what you wanted me to do, and I know I can handle it."

He smiled with a hint of pride in his eyes. He leaned forward, looking at the scattered papers on his desk. "You're right, and I know you can handle it."

I picked up some of the documents I had already gone through. "So the schedule is already set and finalized." I handed him a calendar with times and dates of meetings. He took them and looked over them as I continued speaking. "Before you say anything, I am fully aware of certain things missing. I made the executive decision as your luna and your mate, I deligated some of the responsibilities between Shade and Tristan to take some stress off of you."

He looked back up at me with an expression I couldn't decipher. "That's impressive, you really have been busy while I was gone." He looked back down at the calendar again before looking back up at me. "You made some good decisions. Delegating some of the responsibilities between Tristan and Shade will definitely help to take some of the stress off of me. Well done little one."

I looked at him with uncertainty hidden in my voice. "You aren't mad? I made some pretty big choices without running it by you." Why was I throwing myself under the bus?

He smiled, almost like he wanted to laugh. "Why would I be mad? You made some good decisions… and I appreciate that you took some of the pressure off me. You're doing a great job as luna, and I trust your judgment."

I looked away from him and down at my copy of the calendar. "There's something else that's been bothering me." I looked back up at him.

He raised an eyebrow and looked at me with concern. "What's been bothering you, luna?"

I sighed and handed him the documents I was working on. "I took notice while going through some of the pack documents that we don't start training the pups until they're at least 18. I think it's an oversight and that needs to change…" I took another deep breath. "I organized age ranges and names to form groups I think would work well together, and under either Shade or Ryker I feel they would thrive."

He looked through the documents and seemed to be contemplating the idea I presented. "Training the pups earlier… that's… a good idea." He nodded as he spoke, his eyes still roaming the pages in front of him. "I know Shade is eager to start training the pups as soon as possible, but I don't want to rush things and train them too early."

I adjusted in my seat and leaned forward slightly. "That's why the youngest wouldn't train but get to explore our territory with supervision." I placed my elbows on the desk and leaned against it. "Getting attacked isn't something you plan. If we at least allow the youngest of our pack to familiarize themselves with the area, then we ensure they'll know where to go to escape if the need arises."

He nodded again and took a deep breath, thinking about my suggestion. "That's a good idea, luna... having them explore our territory with supervision is a good way to ensure they're familiar with the area." He paused and continued looking down at the documents, his voice taking on a slightly considerate quality. "But you're right, getting attacked isn't something you plan for... and we can't always protect them." He looked back up at me with a sense of concern. "So it would be best to train them as early as possible."

I couldn't help but smile, I felt like I did something good for the sake of the pack.

Chapter Fifteen

Before we could go over the finer details, Tristan knocked and informed us that the other pack leaders were starting to arrive. I looked back at Greyson. "I guess that's our que."I stood to my feet and took a deep breath. I was a bit nervous about meeting other packs and had no idea what was going to happen, but with Greyson by my side, I knew I'd be okay.

He stood to his feet. "Alright, let's get ready to meet the other pack leaders." He buttoned two of the buttons on the center of his suit jacket. "This is an important meeting… It's essential that we make a good impression." He stepped around his desk and took my hand in his, looking down at me with pride in his eyes. "I have full confidence in you luna, I know you'll do an excellent job." He kissed my forehead and led me out of the office.

I kept with his pace, his shoes and my heels clicking against the floor as we walked over to greet the other pack leaders. He led me down a long hallway and through a large set of wooden doors, where several leaders from neighboring packs were waiting. They're all gathered around a large table, talking and laughing amongst themselves. As soon as they saw Greyson and myself they stopped talking and turned to face us.

My eyes scanned each of the leaders until my eyes came across my parents. I composed myself to the best of my abilities and pried my eyes away from them, pretending that they were anyone else. At the end of it all, they weren't my parents anymore. I turned to Greyson with a smile on my face.

He took in all of the leaders standing around the large wooden table, his voice lightly calm and authoritative. "Hello... thank you all for coming. I'm Greyson, the alpha of this pack for those of you who do not know me. And this is Naphinae, our luna. I hope you all had a safe trip here." He paused for a moment. "We're here to discuss some important matters related to our respective packs... " Greyson led me to a seat and pulled the chair out for me, I nodded at him in appreciation and placed one of my hands over his before he sat down.

He sat down in the chair next to me and looks back at the other leaders, his voice taking on a slightly confident quality as he speaks. "Alright, let's get straight to business. As you know, our packs have had some disagreements in the past... but I believe it's time for us to move forward and find ways to work together." He looks around the table and takes in all of their expressions as they all listened intently.

One of the other pack leaders spoke up. "Hello, alpha Greyson and auna Naphinae." He nodded at us respectively. "I am alpha Skylar of the Black Oak pack, this is my mate and luna, Quinn." He gestured to the woman next to him and she bowed her head in respect as well. "How exactly are we going to be moving forward? Things have been said, wars have taken place."

Greyson smiled and nodded at Skylar. "Hello, alpha Skylar... it's a pleasure to meet you and your luna, Quinn, properly." He took a moment to think on what he would say. "Yes, things have been said and wars have taken place... but I believe we can set all of that aside and focus on the future." He looks around the table again, his voice taking on a slightly considerate quality as he speaks. "We're all stronger together than we are apart..."

Another pack leader chimed in. "Alpha, luna." She nodded respectively as well. "I am luna Hailey of the Lunar pack. How exactly will we move forward? As alpha Skylar has brought to the table, it's a concern. We all have our pups to think of." She leaned forward and crossed her hands as she waited for a response.

Greyson looked at luna Hailey and nodded respectfully. "Hello, luna Hailey... it's nice to meet you as well. Yes, I understand your concern... but there is nothing to worry about." He looked around the table again. "I'm not proposing that we stop protecting our packs or abandon our values... rather, I believe we should work together to ensure everyone is safe."

I sat up a bit straighter and leaned forward placing one of my hands over Greyson's as I looked out amongst the other pack leaders. "I believe that the best way to move forward is to open the conversation as to how we can all build bridges and re-establish a strong relationship. If anyone has anything they'd like to say toward that by all means." I spoke with confidence despite feeling my parents looking at me.

Greyson looked at me and smiled proudly. "I couldn't agree more, luna... opening the conversation and working together is the best way to build strong bridges and establish a relationship." He looks around the table again. "I think we should start by addressing some of our past disagreements... and then move on from there." He paused momentarily and took another deep breath, trying to remain calm.

We carried a long conversation with most of the pack leaders, my parents stood reserved and quiet as they observed the conversation.

I turned my attention to them. "Alpha Alexander, luna Jane." I nodded at them respectfully, and my stomach twisted. They didn't deserve my respect, but I wasn't going to jeopardize this meeting because of their presence. "You've both been rather quiet. Anything either of you would care to comment on?" I couldn't hide the hint of disdain in my tone, although I kept my calm and respective nature.

Greyson looked at my parents, his voice taking on a slightly cautious quality. "Hello, alpha Alexander and luna Jane... it's a pleasure to meet you both. Yes, I did notice that neither of you has said much so far... so I'm curious if there's anything either of you would like to contribute?" He looked back at me with a sense of concern. I balled my hands up on my knees, hidden beneath the table.

"My only concern is as to why you took in an abomination such as our daughter. Are you not aware that your so-called luna is unable to shift?" Alpha Alexander said, his voice drenched in venom.

Greyson looked at Alexander with a sense of concern, his voice defensive. "Alpha Alexander... Luna isn't an abomination, she's our luna... and whether or not she can shift is not important. We don't discriminate against any wolves based on their ability to shift... that would be completely unfair."

My father scoffed. "So the little wolf still can't shift. Poor Naphinae." My fathers words stung like a thousand daggers. It's been over a month since he's seen me and he still holds so much hate in his heart for me. "You should banish her like we did. She's of no use to anyone."

Greyson's eyes reflected a sense of anger and disbelief, his voice taking on a slightly harsh quality as he spoke. "What you did was unforgivable... and I don't care what you have to say about our luna. She's an amazing wolf who is incredibly strong and capable... she's everything we could ask for in our luna. I will not banish her... not now and not ever."

My father stood to his feet with his hands placed on the tabletop and looked at Greyson with pure defiance. "You want your pack to thrive? To build alliances? Then you need to get rid of weakness and she is the biggest one you have."

I slammed my fist against the table and stood to my feet, staring into the eyes of the devil. "I AM MORE CAPABLE THAN YOU EVER GAVE ME CREDIT FOR!" I took a breath and tried to ground myself to avoid an uncontrolled shift. The entire room had their eyes on me.

Rising to his feet, Greyson directed a furious gaze towards Alexander, his voice dripping with contempt. "You have no right to speak to our luna in such a manner..." He stops, composing himself before continuing. "She is no weakling and is no one's weakness. She has worked tirelessly to become the powerful and capable wolf she is today, and I won't tolerate you disrespecting her in such a way."

I could feel my eyes glowing as a low and guttural growl escaped my lips. "It's time you left Father. The Wind Walker Pack will be making no alliances with Crimson Moon for as long as you're in power." I was furious and it showed enough to strike fear into my mother.

Taking a step towards Alexander, Greyson towered over him and stared down at him with intense rage. "I would be careful if I were you... if you keep pushing our patience any further, it won't end well for you." He speaks with a cold fury, his voice dripping with menace.

I sighed and composed myself as best I could. "This meeting is over. For every pack here today besides Crimson Moon, feel free to contact us to schedule another meeting. I sincerely apologize for the behavior displayed here today." I bowed my head a bit ashamed I couldn't hold my anger.

The pack leaders left one by one bowing their heads in respect for Greyson and myself, until it was just my parents left alone with us. He watched as the pack leaders left and showed respect, before turning to face Alexander and Jane.

He spoke with a calm and authoritative quality, his voice no longer dripping with fury. "I'm going to give you two a chance to leave now... but if I ever see you showing our luna such disrespect again, it will not end well for you." He pauses for a moment and takes another deep breath, trying to remain calm despite the anger he was feeling. "Get out." Alexander growled the entire way out my mother following close behind but she seemed more afraid.

Greyson watched them leave with a sense of relief, before turning his attention back to me. He spoke with a gentle and considerate quality to his voice. "Are you alright little one?" he asked as he placed a hand on my shoulder. "I know that had to be difficult for you... but I'm proud of how you handled yourself in there."

I nodded and took a deep breath, trying to calm myself down. "I'm okay." I stood up and turned to face him. "I am so sorry, I feel like I let you down back there. Letting the anger get the better of me like that wasn't okay."

He shook his head and smiled, his voice taking on a slightly encouraging quality. "Don't ever think that... you didn't let me down at all. In fact, I'm proud of how you stood up for yourself. Your father should never have spoken to you that way... I'm just glad you were able to keep your composure until he left."

I smiled up at him. "Thank you."

He smiled back at me. "You're welcome. I'm sorry you had to deal with that… I know it wasn't easy for you. But I want you to know that no matter what happens or who tries to hurt you, I'll always be here for you."

I didn't let him continue. I closed the distance between us and hugged him tightly. "You have no idea how much that means to me."

Wrapping his arms tightly around me and bringing me close, his voice became soft and reassuring. "I'm glad to hear that... because every word I said was sincere." He paused, taking a deep breath to control the emotions that were flooding through him. In a soft voice, he continued. "You are very important to me, luna... and I want you to know just how much I care about you."

I giggled a bit as I nuzzled against him. "Oh please, you're just saying that because you're my mate. You're biased."

He chuckled softly and shook his head, still hugging me tightly as he spoke. "I may be biased, but that doesn't mean I'm wrong. You are an amazing wolf... and you deserve to be loved and appreciated for who you are." He paused. "And whether or not we're mated doesn't change that."

I blushed lightly as I pulled back from the hug to look up at him. "You really mean that?"

He nodded and looked down at me, his voice taking on a slightly reassuring quality as he spoke. "Of course I mean it... you're an amazing wolf who deserves to be loved and appreciated." He brought his hand to my face and caressed my cheekbone lightly with his thumb as he looked into my eyes. "And I want you to know just how much I care about you." He looked into my eyes for a moment, before leaning down and giving me a soft kiss on the lips.

I felt a jolt of warmth and happiness flow through me as he kissed me. I wrapped my arms around him and pulled him closer, deepening the kiss. He returned the passion in the kiss, his body responding instinctively as he pulled me closer. His arms wrapped tightly around me, his heart beating rapidly as he savored the moment. I broke the kiss after a few moments, breathing heavily as I looked into his eyes. I smiled at him, blushing. He looks down at me, his eyes shining brightly with affection. His heart was beating rapidly and he was struggling to control the emotions that were flooding through him. "I'm sorry... I shouldn't have done that." He paused for a moment, before continuing in a soft voice. "But I couldn't help myself... you're just so beautiful and amazing."

I giggled and placed my hands on his chest, adjusting his tie. "Okay hot shot, calm down."

He chuckled softly and looked down at me, the corners of his mouth turning up in a smile. He wraps his arms around me, pulling me close once again. "You think I'm a hot shot?" He says in a playful tone. "If you really want me to calm down, maybe you should give me something else to think about... Something like... another kiss?"

I broke out into full-blown laughter. "Nice try, but I think that'll have the opposite effect." I leaned my head against his chest and just enjoyed being held.

He chuckled softly, his voice taking on a slightly affectionate quality as he spoke. "Oh come on... I was just kidding. Well, sort of... Just give me one more kiss and I'll be good." He looked down at me with a smile, his eyes shining brightly with affection.

I didn't even look up at him. "You're giving me puppy dog eyes aren't you?"

He laughed softly and shook his head. "Maybe... but is it working?" His voice was filled with affection, his eyes glinting with mischief as he spoke.

I looked up at him grinning from ear to ear, my eyes searching his. "You aren't going to give up, are you?"

He looks at me with a smile, the corners of his mouth turning up in amusement. "Nope... I'm not giving up until I get that kiss." His voice was playful but firm, a look of determination on his face.

I rolled my eyes playfully. "Okay, okay." I leaned up and rested my hand against the back of his neck, pulling him down to me gently.

His heart was racing as he leaned in, his body responding instinctively as our lips met. The kiss was passionate and intense, his hands moving to the small of my back as he held me close.

In the heat of the moment, I could feel his inner wolf stirring, urging him to claim me as his mate. As the kiss deepened, I could feel him being swept away by his inner wolf... he was overcome with a primal and intense desire to claim me. His hands moved down to my waist, pulling me even closer as his lips continued to move against mine. I felt a warning in the back of my head, urging me to pull away but I couldn't bring myself to. His hands tightened against my waist as the kiss started to grow into something hungry and driven by an intense lust. I could feel his inner wolf trying to assert dominance, trying to claim. I could feel his inner wolf struggling against mine, fighting for dominance.

I could sense the primal urges coursing through him, his inner wolf taking control of him. I could feel the bond forming, the connection between us growing stronger with each passing moment. His lips continued to move against mine, his hunger growing like a forest fire. I couldn't fight against the feeling either but my mind wouldn't allow me to surrender to it either. I could feel the heat building, the raw emotions taking over us both.

I finally snapped to my senses and pulled away. "Woah, Grey. Calm down." I backed up and gave him some space, holding my hands flat out in the air.

He looked at me with a confused expression, his voice taking on a slightly confused quality as he spoke. "Calm down? What do you mean?" He paused for a moment and took a deep breath, trying to control the emotions that were flooding through him. "I... I don't understand. Why are you pulling away?" He took another deep breath, trying to stay calm despite the confusion and frustration that he was feeling.

I tried to find the right words to explain to him but felt the overwhelming urge to just run away. He watched me, his eyes glittering with confusion.

His voice took on a slightly frustrated quality as he spoke. "Why do you keep backing away? What did I do wrong?" He paused momentarily and took a deep breath, trying to stay calm.

I took a deep breath and tried to gather my thoughts. "It's just… I… I don't know how to explain it… I'm just not ready for...this."

He looked at me with a hint of disappointment, his voice taking on a slightly resentful quality as he spoke. "You're not ready? We've been mates for months... I thought you were ready. I thought... that you wanted this too."

My stomach turned at the familiar expression on his face. "Grey…"

I struggled to find my words and ultimately looked down at the ground feeling disappointed in myself.

His voice took on a slightly harsher tone as he spoke. "Don't "Grey..." me. If you're not ready, then you should have said something sooner. I... I thought this was what you wanted too." He sounded hurt and confused.

"It was just... I was scared... scared of what it might mean, what it would change between us." My voice cracked a bit, my eyes still fixated at the ground beneath me.

He paused for a moment. "Scared? What are you afraid of?" He sounded concerned, his voice taking on a softer and more gentle quality as he spoke. "You're my mate... I love you. And no matter what happens or who tries to hurt you, I'll always be there for you." His voice was filled with genuine affection and concern as he spoke.

I closed my eyes and took a deep breath. "I hear you, I do. I... I'm still new to all of this." I brushed my hand up my arm, suddenly feeling small and vulnerable.

His voice took on a soothing quality as he spoke. "I understand... and I'm sorry if I pressured you. I just thought... that you felt the same way." He paused momentarily and took another deep breath, trying to control his emotions. "But if you don't want this yet... then that's okay." His voice was filled with concern and compassion as he spoke.

Despite his kind words of reassurance, I heard him walk past me and leave me in the meeting room alone. I opened my eyes and he was gone. I sat down in a chair and held my head in my hands. I sighed deeply and leaned back in the chair, my thoughts clouded with confusion and frustration. "Why did I do that?" I murmured to myself, feeling the weight of my own actions on my shoulders. I couldn't help but feel like I had made a mistake, and I wondered if things would ever be the same between us again.

I sat there for a few more minutes trying to shake the disappointed look on his face from my mind. I couldn't... I got up and walked back to the bedroom we had been sharing, my heels clicking against the hardwood floors of the pack house. 'Don't cry.' I repeated in my head, over, and over, and over again. I got into our room and sat on the bed quickly kicking off my heels. I took another moment to pull myself together, but I couldn't hold her back anymore. My wolf was knocking on the front door of my mind, begging, pleading for control. I needed to get out of this dress, I couldn't reach the zipper and I started to feel a sense of panic. I fought back every primal urge I was faced with. After a few minutes of struggling, I gave up on the zipper and tore the dress off.

With the dress off, I finally gave in to my urges and my shift started. My bones breaking echoed off the walls of the bedroom. It stung, but the pain was numbing in comparison to what I was feeling already. After I finished my shift and stood on all four of my paws, I bolted from the pack house and into the forest outside. I caught the attention of some of the other pack members, but I didn't care. I felt free…

I spent hours running through the pack's territory. The wind ruffled through my fur. It felt lonely running alone, no Shade, no Greyson. I needed this though, with or without anyone there with me.

Once my legs grew tired enough, I made my way back to the pack house. I wasn't ready to face what happened but I knew I had to. I trotted back into the bedroom Greyson and I shared and focused on shifting back. Being this tired made it hurt like hell. I didn't bother with clothes, I showered briefly to get the dirt off and dried off before throwing myself into our bed. I was alone in bed, in the room in general. I tried to wait for him but the exhaustion I felt was too much and I ended up falling asleep with a heavy heart.

Chapter Sixteen

Sleep was blissful until it wasn't. I started reliving my childhood in my sleep. The memories of my siblings making great strides in the pack and me getting left behind as 'the abomination' my parents always claimed I was. My father's constant verbal and sometimes physical abuse.

I could feel myself crying in my sleep, I was trapped in a moment of hell. Stuck reliving the worst memories I had of my family. My mind begged and pleaded for it to stop. I could feel my surroundings but I couldn't open my eyes. My face wet with tears that have escaped me. I couldn't wake up. Images of my father hitting me and telling me I wasn't worth it, that I wasn't good enough. I could feel myself sobbing, I clung to the pillow closest to me.

All I had to do was open my eyes and it would be over, but I couldn't. It was agony…

My sobs grew louder and more agonizing as the worst memory of them all flooded my mind and I was completely submerged and immersed in the moment. My father had me tied to a tree with my back stripped and bare. My youngest sibling, Anne, broke the thing my father held most valuable. My grandmother's urn and her ashes alongside it, broken and scattered against the floor. Like a good older sister, I took the blame. My father didn't hold back.

His demeaning words fell away as the whip he held sliced through the air and the unmistakable sound of the crack it produced echoed through the trees. I could feel my skin tearing away with each lash my blood running hot against the cold of my broken skin.

I screamed out as if the pain I was feeling was happening to me outside of the memory. I lay in bed crying and clinging to the pillow I had as if my life depended on it as the memory played through my mind like a broken record. Every time my father's whip lashed against my back in the memory was every time I screamed out, reliving every ounce of pain as if I was feeling it for the first time.

I wasn't just crying anymore, I was shaking from fear, and my bones were rattling. I was sweating from the amount of pain I was reliving and how hard I was fighting to wake up. I could feel the pain radiating throughout my body, both physically and emotionally. My body was covered in sweat and I couldn't escape from my mind.

I tried to break away from the dream, but it felt like I was stuck in a quicksand with no hope for escape. My heart was racing and I felt like I couldn't catch my breath. I screamed out in my dream, feeling like my body was being ripped apart from the inside out. I could feel the nightmare taking over, like a vicious cycle that I couldn't break.

I felt his touch on my arm and my eyes fluttered open, the nightmare finally breaking away.

I looked up at him with tears streaming down my face. "Grey?" My voice was hoarse from screaming. He nodded and wiped away my tears. He didn't say anything but I could see in his eyes something was wrong. Besides still feeling shaken from reliving my past, my heart broke for him. I took a deep breath so my voice would be solid and not as shaky as I felt. "Are… are you okay?" He nodded again, but I could see in his eyes he was hurting too.

I appreciated him trying to put me first, but I didn't want him in pain either. "You're lying. You're quiet and you're lying. What's wrong?" I didn't move, it didn't feel like I should.

He seemed surprised that I could see through him so easily. I watched as his mask slipped and he took a deep breath, his vulnerability starting to shine through his rough demeanor. "I… I wanted to comfort you so badly, but I had to stay in control."

I furrowed my eyebrows, so much so I swear they knitted together. "Stay in control? I don't understand."

He took another deep breath and tried to explain. "When I… when I tried to comfort you, my wolf tried to take control." He paused for a moment, wanting me to understand. "My wolf… it wants you." His face flushed with embarrassment, knowing that he had just admitted something very vulnerable to me. He visibly felt ashamed of himself, but he couldn't lie to me.

I shook my head, my eyebrows still knitted together. "I'm sorry, forgive my naivety. I still don't understand."

He broke eye contact and looked away from me like he was trying to find the right words. "My wolf… it wants you as my mate." He took a moment and looked back at me suddenly speaking frantically like he had to explain himself further. "But my wolf doesn't control me, I do. I could never force you to be my mate if you don't want me to."

My eyebrows finally relaxed. "Greyson Carver… I didn't get scared because I don't want to be your mate." I felt tears well up in my eyes again. I looked straight up at the ceiling and took a deep breath before speaking again. I looked back down and my eyes met his. "I was scared you'd regret it one day. I was scared that… a permanent bond to me… it wouldn't hold that… that you'd find better in someone else…" I started to break up my sentence with short breaths trying to fight back my tears. I looked up at the ceiling trying to keep my tears at bay.

"Look at me Naphinae." His voice was gentle and reassuring. I looked at him, my tears threatening to fall. "I have no interest in any other woman. You are all that I want, all that I need." He paused for a moment looking into my eyes, searching for the right words. "You are everything to me." I bit the inside of my cheek trying so desperately not to cry. He put his finger under my chin and gently lifted it up… wanting me to look him in the eyes. "It's okay, you don't have to hold back your tears. If I could take away all of the pain that you have felt… if I could give you a life full of happiness…" His voice was soft and sincere, wanting to reassure me that I didn't need to be afraid anymore. I was safe with him.

I couldn't fight my tears anymore. As they fell, I threw myself into his arms sobbing like a baby. I clung to him, holding him tightly. The home I never knew I needed, the sense of belonging, it was never the pack… It was him. He is where I belong.

He wrapped his arms tightly around me. "Shh… it's okay, you can let it all out."

I couldn't stop crying, it was like a dam had been broken. I let it all out, the pain, the hurt, the anger, the fear. All of it came pouring out of me like a waterfall. I cried and cried, clinging to him tightly.

After a while of crying into his embrace, I pulled back. I'm sure I looked like a complete wreck. "Will it hurt?" I held on to his arms for support as I sat up.

He seemed surprised by my sudden shift in demeanor. "Will what hurt?"

I wiped my eyes and looked up at him. "Being claimed... Will it hurt?" I was nervous, but I wanted this, needed this. I needed him.

He paused for a moment, trying to find the right words. "No... it won't hurt. It might feel strange at first, but once you get used to it... it will feel natural." He smiled and ran his hand through my hair, trying to reassure me. "Being claimed by your mate is one of the most intimate and sacred experiences in our world." He paused for a moment, looking into my eyes. "And I would never do anything to harm you."

I nodded and took a deep breath. I knew I was ready to take the next step. "What happens now?"

He took a deep breath and then smiled. "First, I have to mark you as my mate." He paused for a moment, wanting to explain the process clearly. "To do this... I will bite you... right here." He pointed to his neck just below his ear. "It will hurt at first, but the pain will quickly fade and it won't hurt anymore." He paused for a moment, wanting to make sure that I understood what he was about to do. "Are you ready?"

I looked up at him a bit more nervously. "You said it wouldn't hurt."

He sighed and nodded, wanting to reassure me. "The pain is only temporary... once you're marked, it will never hurt again. I know this is a big decision..." He looked into my eyes. "But I promise you that it's worth it..." His voice was soft and gentle, wanting to help calm my nerves.

I was unsure of a lot of things, but my feelings toward this, toward him, it was one of the only things I was sure of. "You've... marked me before. What makes this different?"

He smiled at me. His smile was so genuine and so warm it could melt the arctic. "Claiming a mate fully can take many forms. For an alpha and luna, it's intimate and powerful, but most of all... we can mark each other as many times as we like, claiming is acceptance, complete acceptance."

I nodded, taking a deep breath. "I'm ready." He smiled and then slowly leaned in towards my neck, feeling the heat of his breath against my skin.

He paused for a moment, wanting to make sure that this was what I wanted. "Are you sure?" he whispered softly, wanting to give me one last chance to change my mind.

I nodded, feeling the warmth of his breath against my neck. I closed my eyes and waited for the pain to come. Despite my best efforts to remain calm, I was still trembling like a leaf. He knew I was afraid, but I wanted this. I wasn't going to run, not after everything.

"I'm so sorry…" he whispered softly. He bit down on my neck quickly, his teeth sinking into my skin and breaking through with little effort. I flinched at the sudden pain, biting down on my lip to prevent a scream from escaping my lips.

The pain was intense and sharp, but I didn't make a sound, knowing that this was a necessary step in our journey together.

He continued to bite down on my neck, his teeth sinking deeper into my skin. In the midst of the pain, I couldn't help but feel grateful for him. I knew that he was doing this out of love, that he was marking me as his mate for life.

Closing my eyes tightly, I tried to block out the pain and focus on the sensation of being marked by him. The feeling was unlike anything I had ever experienced before, it was both painful and exhilarating. The pain was a lot to endure and it felt like it was never-ending. I slowly felt my body going limp in his arms, I clung to consciousness as hard as I could. My eyes began to flutter and I did my best to stay awake. I looked up at him, tears streaming down my face, as he continued to bite down on my neck. I tried to focus on the feeling, trying to block out the pain.

He held me tighter as he bit down at his hardest.

I finally felt the sharp pain subside, replaced by a warm and comforting feeling. I looked up at him, tears still streaming down my face. I was a part of him now. He pulled back and looked down at me, concern filled his blue eyes. As much pain as I was in, it was overridden by love, genuine love.

His eyes softened as his concern remained. "How do you feel?"

Honestly I felt a bit dazed and unfocused, but I was okay. I felt different... like I was now a part of something bigger than myself. I felt a sense of peace and belonging that I had never felt before.

I looked up at him, tears still streaming down my face, and whispered, "I feel complete."

He smiled and pulled me back into him, hugging me tightly. "I'm glad." He pulled away just enough to look down at me. He brushed my stray hair from my face and looked into my eyes as he spoke. "You are mine now... I'll protect you, care for you... Always." He paused for a moment and kissed my forehead. "And I'll love you... Always."

I smiled softly and leaned into his touch, feeling comforted by his presence. "I know..." I whispered softly, feeling like I had finally found my place in this world.

He smiled and gently lifted my chin so that I was looking him in the eyes. "From now on, you will always have me." He paused for a moment, trying reassure me. "You don't have to be afraid of anything anymore..." His voice was gentle and soothing.

I am home now, Greyson Carver is my home.

I looked up at him a bit unsure. "Do I have to do that to you too?"

He smiled softly down at me. "If you want to then yes, but there's no pressure..." He ran his fingers through my hair. "It's up to you... Whatever you decide, I will respect your choice."

I looked down and thought for a moment before looking back up at him and I nodded. "I want to, but I don't want to hurt you."

He smiled and stroked my hair as he spoke. "It won't hurt... not for very long. I promise." I nodded, still unsure but willing to try.

He gently guided my head back, exposing his neck to me. "Go ahead... It's not going to hurt." He trusted me.

In this moment it felt as if both of our masks were gone, we were both vulnerable in front of one another. I was scared but I needed to do this. I took a deep breath and moved a bit closer to him. I wrapped my arms around him, hugging him tightly. I kissed his neck first, trying to express how sorry I was for the pain I was about to cause him, then bit down softly at first but bit down harder gradually until I could taste his blood.

He groaned softly as I bit harder. He closed his eyes and took a deep breath as he allowed his body to relax. I felt guilty knowing this hurt, but I proceeded for as long as he'd let me. I bit down at my hardest and held him tightly hoping it would ease some of the pain. He remained still the entire time, allowing me to do this despite the pain I knew he was feeling. I felt like I was doing something wrong as if I was hurting him more than I should. He was so understanding and patient with me, despite the pain I was currently causing him.

I finally stopped, my heart racing. I looked up at him, eyes wide, afraid of what he might think.

"I'm okay... don't worry about me. That was..." He took a deep breath, trying to find the right words. "It was painful... but it wasn't as bad as I thought it would be. And it was worth it..." He smiled and gently caressed my cheek. I looked into his eyes, seeing the pain in them and I felt horrible for hurting him. He tried to reassure me that it was okay. "Don't worry about me... I knew what I was getting myself into when I claimed you." He brushed the hair out of my face and gently caressed my cheek. "This pain is nothing compared to the happiness I feel now... being with you." His voice was soft and soothing, everything was going to be okay.

I sighed deeply. "But still, I'm sorry for the pain I've caused you."

He shook his head. "You have nothing to be sorry for... I don't regret it for a second." He held my face in his hand, making sure I was looking directly at him when he spoke. "Being with you is worth any pain that I might feel..."

In this moment I knew, and I've never been more sure. "I love you, Greyson Carver. Mind, body, and soul... I love you."

He smiled and gently pulled me closer, wanting to hold me tightly. "I love you too... more than you could ever imagine." He paused for a moment, wanting to make sure that I understood what he meant. "You are my whole world... my heart, my soul, my everything." He kissed me softly on the forehead and then gently caressed my cheek. "And I will always protect you... no matter what."

I looked up at him and cupped his face, bringing him closer and resting my forehead against his. "I know I've said it before, but know this… I have never meant something more in my life than I do right now."

He smiled and gently kissed me on the forehead. "I know... I love you too, more than you could ever imagine." He kissed me softly on the lips, not wanting to let go of this moment with me. "And I will never let anything or anyone hurt you." He held me tightly, wanting to make sure that I knew how much I meant to him.

I looked into his eyes, his beautifully broken blue eyes. I leaned my head against his shoulder and just enjoyed being close to him in this moment, our moment.

He smiled and wrapped his arms tighter around me, wanting to hold me close. "You know... you're the most beautiful girl I've ever seen. And I'm the luckiest guy in the world to have you as my mate." He leaned down and kissed me softly on the forehead.

I giggled, "There you go again, being biased."

He smiled and brushed the hair out of my face. "Maybe I am a little biased... but it's still true. You're the most beautiful girl in the world to me... and I wouldn't want anyone else as my mate."

I rested my hand against his chest and my giggle became a laugh as I playfully rolled my eyes. "Biased."

He laughed, "Just a little..." He paused for a moment. "You're not just my mate, you're my best friend and the love of my life." He kissed me softly on the forehead and then gently caressed my cheek. "And I will never love anyone as much as I love you." I giggled again, my smile had never felt more genuine.

I took a breath from all the laughter. "Okay, okay. So now that we've officially marked each other, what happens now?"

He paused, thinking. "Well... now that we've marked each other... we're bound together." He paused for a moment, trying to find his words. "It's like... our souls have become intertwined." He gently caressed my cheek. "We'll always be connected... no matter where we are or what happens, we'll always be with each other."

I sat up and held his hands in mine. "No special abilities? Although I was already able to feel your pain and lean on your strength, I'd assume that capability is stronger now." I moved one of my hands from his to the mark he left on my neck.

He watched my hand move to the mark. "Well..." He paused again. "There are some special abilities that come with being marked... but it's not something that happens right away." He squeezed my hand gently. "But eventually, you'll start to feel more connected to me... and I'll start to feel more connected to you." He kissed me softly on the cheek.

Chapter Seventeen

"Grey, can I ask you something?"

He paused for a moment, wondering what I wanted to ask him. "Of course you can... what's on your mind?" He looked at me and waited for me to ask my question.

I looked up at him nervously, I was unsure of what his reaction would be. "You... you never talk about your family. I know that Tristan and Teagan are twins, and they're your younger siblings..." I looked down and took a deep breath, taking both his hands in mine again as I played with our fingers together. "But what about your parents? What happened to them?"

His entire demeanor shifted, I could tell this wasn't a topic he enjoyed talking about. "Well..." He took a deep breath before talking again. "My parents... they were killed when I was young." He looked down at our hands. "Tristan and Teagan were there too... but they survived."

I looked at him, surprised and saddened by his answer. I reached out and gently touched his shoulder. I wanted to comfort him, to let him know that I was there for him.

He looked back up at me and saw the sympathy in my eyes. "Don't worry about me..." He paused for a moment, trying to find his words. "My parents would have wanted me to be happy... and they would have wanted me to find someone like you." He gently squeezed my hands and kissed them softly. "You make me happy, Little One... so please don't feel bad for me."

I shook my head and could feel my eyes welling up with tears. "Grey, I am so sorry. I didn't mean to bring up painful memories."

He smiled and wiped away my tears. "It's okay. It was a long time ago, and I've made my peace with it... Thank you for caring about me." He kissed my forehead, resting his hand against the back of my neck.

"I shouldn't have asked, I should've let you talk about it when you were ready. That wasn't fair of me." I looked at him as he sat back down. "You gave me the time to open up and didn't pry about my family or my childhood. I should've done the same." I shook my head and looked down at my hands. I was feeling guilty for bringing up his past.

"No... it's fine. I don't blame you... you were just curious." He smiled and gently lifted my head up so that I was looking him in the eyes. "And besides... talking about this isn't easy for me... but I wanted you to know the truth." He brushed the hair out of my face.

"And I appreciate that you opened up to me too... I feel like I know you better now." I mumbled to him. "I don't want to hurt you anymore."

He looked at me, noticing how I was feeling guilty for hurting him. "You didn't hurt me..." He paused for a moment, shaking his head with a smile plastered on his face as if he wanted to laugh. "Yes, the bite was painful... but it was worth it. And I would do it again in a heartbeat." He kissed me softly on the forehead and then caressed my cheek. "You could never hurt me... not intentionally anyway." He gently squeezed my hand and smiled at me, a small chuckle escaped him.

I looked down again and took a moment to think about what I was going to say and if I was fully ready, I was. "It's only fair. Ask me whatever you want, no matter how emotionally painful." I looked back up at him determined.

He looked at me confused. "Are you sure? I don't want to make you feel bad..." He rubbed his hand over my shoulder. "Are you ready for me to ask about your past?"

I knew he didn't want to force me into anything, but I felt I had to do this. I nodded my head and gave him a small smile. "Ask me anything." I placed my hand over his, on my shoulder.

He hesitated for a moment. "Okay… What happened with your parents?" His voice was soft like he didn't really want to ask.

"Do you mean what happened at the pack leaders meeting yesterday?"

He nodded his head and looked at me, waiting for me to answer the question. "Yes… But I meant more in general. What happened to your parents? Why aren't you living with them anymore?" he asked softly, wanting to hear my side of the story.

I took a moment to think about how to answer his question. I felt angry and sad, but it wasn't because of his question. "My parents… They never really loved me the way you should love and nurture a child. I'm the oldest of five siblings and for them to see my siblings thrive while I couldn't even manage my first shift… I became the abomination of the Crimson moon pack."

He listened to my words carefully, his mind processing as I spoke. "So they never really loved you? That must've been hard for you… growing up with parents who didn't love or accept you." He squeezed my hand gently as his other hand came up and rested against my face. "But I think you're amazing… and I can't imagine why anyone would see you as an abomination."

I took a moment before continuing. "My father was abusive. He never cared about me the way he did with the rest of his children. They were all his pride and joy, and I was treated as a stain on his reputation as alpha."

He looked angry at the thought of what I was saying being true. "That's not right… no child should have to grow up with an abusive parent. What about your mother? Did she ever stand up for you?"

I shook my head. "Unfortunately, she stood by my father's choice blindly. The only time she's ever seemed to care about his reaction toward me was when my father banished me from the Crimson Moon pack." I watched as his eyes widened.

"So she let your father banish you from the pack? She didn't even try to stop him?" I stood silent trying to gather my thoughts, but he was more curious about my past than I had anticipated. "So they never loved you… and when you didn't fit their expectations, they banished you. Did they ever come looking for you or did they just cut off all ties with you?"

I smiled at the memory briefly. I looked down for a moment at our hands, the way they fit so perfectly together. I looked back up at him and I could feel a weird sensation and I knew it was our bond. "I had been banished, yes. My parents didn't come looking for me, instead, they let me go and pretended I never existed, assuming they'd never see me again. It hurt at first, but in the week I was alone hiding out in the forest seeking refuge. I had never felt so free." It seemed like he could feel what I was feeling, the rush from our bond.

"I can't imagine how hard that must've been for you… to be cast out by your parents like that." He looked at me, almost as if he was studying my face. "But I'm glad that you found freedom, and that you were able to find your true pack with us." He squeezed my hand again.

"A part of me is thankful they banished me. I don't get to see my siblings grow and find happiness the way I have and that hurts, but they're strong. I know they'll be okay… If it wasn't for my banishment, you never would've found me, and I wouldn't have found my home in you."

He looked at me and smiled. "I'm glad too... You deserve so much more than what your parents gave you..." He gently brushed the hair out of my face and caressed my cheek. "But now you have a pack that loves and supports you... and that's something no one can ever take away from you."

Smiling, I held his hand tightly. "It's amazing how much can change in a week, huh?"

He nodded his head and smiled at me. "It's true... it feels like it was just yesterday that you were a scared, lost wolf... and now you're my mate. You've made such an impact on my life... and I'm forever grateful for that." He squeezed my hand gently and kissed it softly.

Taking a moment, he leaned forward and kissed me softly on the lips. It was gentle, yet held so much meaning. He pulled away and looked at me, feeling a rush of emotions as our lips touched. "I love you, Little One… I love you more than anything... and I will always be here for you." He gently squeezed my hand and then pulled me close, holding me tightly.

I nuzzled against him, resting my head against his chest. I hadn't realized how tired I was until the steady rhythm of his heart beating beneath my ear began to ease the tension I hadn't known I was building.

Greyson sat back against the headboard, allowing me to rest against him as he ran his fingers through my hair. "It's okay… you can rest now…" He kissed the top of my head and squeezed me in a warm hug briefly before returning his hand to run through my hair. "I'm here for you… and I'll always be here for you…" He held me tightly against him. My eyes fluttered shut as the feeling of safety and protection radiated from him.

That was the first time I ever fell asleep without a nightmare taking over my subconscious.

The security Greyson provided for me was unlike anything I'd ever known.

Chapter Eighteen

When I woke up, I was alone in bed again. I knew Greyson was close by. Not only could I smell his scent… I could feel him, his presence, his energy.

"Grey?" I couldn't tell how close he was, just that he wasn't too far. I heard him shuffling around a room or two away, he came back over to the bedroom and stood in the doorway for a moment.

"Little one, is that you?" He sounded worried. "I'm here… are you okay?"

I sat up and groaned, holding my neck as I did. My mark was a bit sore but I think I was okay. "How long was I asleep?"

He walked further into the bedroom. "Only a few hours." I watched his eyes stray from mine and look at my hand on my neck. "Is your mark bothering you?"

I nodded, keeping my hand over it. "Yeah, but nothing to be worried about. It's just a bit sore, but I'm okay I promise." I tilted my head and winced giving him a very unconvincing smile.

He walked over to me with a smirk on his face and brushed my hair away from my neck. "I think I can help with that… Can I take a look at your mark?" He sat next to me and I nodded as I put my hair up in a very sloppy bun. He chuckled at my attempt to put my hair up and got up, moving behind me. "Here, let me help." He took my hair down from how I had it and braided my hair neatly, not a strand out of place.

Once he finished he came back around and sat next to me again. "Let me see your mark little one…" He gave me the moment to be comfortable in showing it to him.

I adjusted how I was sitting and tilted my head so he could see it better, causing myself to whimper at the sudden movement. "Don't move little one… you might hurt yourself if you move too suddenly." He moved my braid over my shoulder opposite my mark. "Can I touch it?"

I looked down realizing I had a shirt on now, I didn't remember getting dressed. "Yeah, I trust you."

He touched my mark, sending a rush through me. "I feel it… I feel our bond is getting stronger."

I wanted to nod but it hurt to even attempt. "I feel it too." He looked up at me. "Is it alright if I try something?"

I admired the amount of caution he took in not wanting to hurt me. "Yes. As long as you aren't going to bite me again." I giggled to break the tension.

He laughed with me. "I promise I won't bite you again… unless you ask me to. But what if I try something different? Would you be okay with that?"

I felt his hands on my shoulders and I turned to face him. "What did you have in mind?"

"Well..." He paused for a moment, thinking about how to explain it. "You know how our bonds work... we share emotions, we feel each other's pain, and we can communicate even without speaking." He looked at me and smiled softly. "I was wondering if I could try to make our bond stronger... not by hurting you, but by sharing more of myself with you. Can I do that?" he asked softly, wanting to make sure I was comfortable with the idea.

I was a bit shocked. "I'm sorry, did you say we could communicate without speaking?"

He nodded his head. "Yes... that's one of the things about being mates. We can communicate without speaking... we can even feel each other's emotions." He paused for a moment, trying to find his words to better explain. "But there's more... we can also share our thoughts and memories with each other." He gently touched my mark again. "Would you be okay with that?" he asked softly.

I was stunned. "So, you could share memories with me? Even memories you'd rather not remember?" I asked, hoping to understand.

He nodded his head as he looked at me. "Yes... if you want me to.

But it's up to you. I don't want to make you feel uncomfortable or put too much pressure on you." He gently touched my mark again, rubbing it lightly. "We don't have to do this if you don't want to," he said softly, wanting me to feel safe and in control of the situation.

In a hushed voice, I confessed, "I have nightmares sometimes..."

His expression became more concerned. "Nightmares? What about? Is it about... your parents?" he asked softly, wanting to be there for me and help however he could.

I nodded, it hurt. "About my father..."

The way he looked at me expressed a mutual pain, telling me he was using our bond. "I'm sorry... I know what it's like to have nightmares about your past." He held my hand a bit tighter. "If you want me to ... I can share some of my happy memories with you... so that they can help replace the bad ones..."

I shook my head. "I don't think anything can ever really make it go away... Was the memory sharing what you wanted to try to make my mark stop hurting?" I raised an eyebrow curious if there was another way to help the pain go away.

He smiled. "Yes... memory sharing is one of the things I wanted to try." He wanted to make sure that he explained it clearly. "When we share memories with each other, it's like reliving them together... but you won't feel the same pain." He gently touched my mark again, as he tried to comfort me. "Would you be okay with trying that?" he asked softly, wanting to help me.

I thought about it for a couple of minutes. "You said one of, what else did you have in mind?"

He chuckled slightly but nodded. "We could go for a run, it might take your mind off of it. Unless there was something else you wanted to do?"

I rubbed my hand over my mark, wincing as I did. "What if we went out? We never did go on that first date... it doesn't have to be fancy."

His face instantly lit up. I didn't need the mate bond to know he was excited over the idea. "You want to go on a date with me? Are you sure? I don't want you to feel like you have to do this..."

I giggled at his rambling and turned to face him properly. I cupped his face with both of my hands. "Greyson Carver, I love you. Me wanting to go on a date with you isn't out of obligation. I want to, unless you're implying you don't." My tone came out more teasing than anything else and I couldn't help but giggle.

"I... of course I want to go on a date with you. In fact..." he said softly, smiling at me as he looked into my eyes. "You can be in charge of picking the place and the time." He gently caressed my cheek. "Whatever makes you happy makes me happy."

I laughed and covered my mouth feeling my face flush with embarrassment. "No pressure."

He smiled and gently took my hand, pulling me closer to him. "Trust me... there's no pressure here. We can do whatever you want, whenever you want." He leaned in and kissed me softly on the lips. "All I care about is making you happy..." he said softly, wanting to make sure that I knew how much he cared for me.

"Grey, I don't care where we go or what we do. I just want to spend time with you." I looked him in the eyes as I spoke.

"Well... there's one place that I've wanted to take you for a while now..." He paused for a moment, wanting to make sure that he got the timing right. "But it's up to you." He caressed my cheek. "Whatever you want to do is fine with me." He kissed my cheek softly and then held me close.

I leaned against him, enjoying him being this close to me and the way he held me like I was the only thing that mattered. "What did you have in mind?"

He looked at me smiling. "Well..." He took a moment. "There's this place that I go to when I need some time to relax and unwind. It's kind of hard to describe it... but it's a special spot that means a lot to me." He gently caressed my cheek and kissed my forehead. "Would you like me to take you there?" he asked softly, wanting my opinion on the idea.

In response, I leaned in to kiss him softly on the lips, feeling the connection between us grow even stronger. When we finally pulled away, I smiled softly, "Yes, please."

When we finally pulled away, he smiled at me and gently caressed my cheek. "Okay then... let me get ready and we can go." He stopped himself from getting off the bed and turned back to face me. "It's kind of a drive though... are you okay with that?" he asked softly, wanting to know if I felt up for it.

I looked at him feeling a bit stunned. "I didn't know you could drive, let alone that you had a car…" I looked down suddenly realizing I really didn't know much about Greyson.

He laughed and held my face in his hand. "I have a Jeep in the garage that I drive around when I need time to myself. Is that okay with you?" There was a silence that lingered.

I looked at him and blinked profusely. "I'm sorry, you said you have a Jeep?! How am I just now hearing about this?" I was completely stunned. "How the fuck are you this perfect? And how did I not find you sooner, because… Holy fuck!"

He laughed at my reaction, making me blush automatically. "Yes… I have a Jeep. Do you want to go check it out? We can go now if you want."

I didn't give it a second thought, I scrambled off the bed. I fell flat on my ass but got up and ran into the closet to grab some pants.

He couldn't contain his laughter. "You okay?" he shouted between laughing at me. "Do you want me to help you put your pants on?" He continued laughing as he walked into the closet.

I couldn't help but join in at laughing at myself. I shook my head. "No, I can handle it. Although I'm pretty sure I bruised my tailbone."

He came closer and placed his hand on my lower back. "Let me take a look…" His hand inched down, feeling his way down my back toward my tailbone. "Does this hurt?"

I couldn't focus on the pain with his hand on me like this. I tried to shake the sensation and focus on literally anything else, I didn't need him knowing he was turning me on, especially with the mate bond there to give me away completely.

"I… I'll be okay."

He gently ran his fingers over my tailbone causing him to wince. "Does this feel better?" Taking a moment in between him speaking again, I knew the mate bond was giving me away. "Do you want me to keep touching it?" His voice took a curious quality. "Or do you want me to stop?"

I shivered and pulled my pants up, snapping myself out of it as I stepped away from him. "I think I'll survive a bruise." I cleared my throat and looked away from him as I felt my face heat up.

He laughed a little harder at my reaction this time. "Yeah… I think you'll be fine too. Do you mind if I keep my hand there for a few more seconds? It should help numb it a little bit…" He stepped closer but didn't touch me. "Only if you want me to though."

I nodded and bit my lip as I tried not to let my emotions show. "Yeah, that's fine." He gently ran his fingers over my tailbone, making me flinch a bit at the unexpected touch. "Sorry."

He continued rubbing my tailbone lightly, the tension releasing slowly. "Does that feel better?" He spoke softly. "Do you want me to keep touching you… Or do you want me to stop?" The idea of his hand continuing to touch my tailbone made me shiver.

"Oh, that felt so much better. Yeah, you can keep your hand there, it helps."

He kept his hand in place. "Good… Let me know if you want me to stop…" The idea of him touching me in such a familiar way made me feel things I couldn't quite put into words. I felt warm and safe with him. "Just let me know if I need to adjust my hand… Do you think this'll help?" His words were soothing.

I stepped closer to him and leaned my head against his chest as I wrapped my arms around him. "It feels better, thank you."

He wrapped his arms around me and pulled me closer, holding me tightly against his chest as he gently caressed my back. He let out a deep breath. "You're welcome..." he said softly.

I relaxed into his embrace as he tightened his hold on me. He rubbed my back as his other hand moved from my tailbone to run his fingers through my hair. "Are you okay now?" I nodded silently and hugged him tighter, my senses overwhelmed by his scent. He hugged me back just as tightly as we stood there together in silence.

He leaned down and gently kissed the top of my head, feeling our bodies press up against each other. He let out a deep breath wanting to hold onto this moment for as long as we could. I nestled into his embrace, closing my eyes and savoring the feeling of his touch.

"Are you ready to go now?" he asked softly. I nodded and looked up at him smiling as I took his hand in mine. He squeezed my hand lightly and kissed it. "Let's go then." He smiled at me and then started walking to the door, still holding my hand as I followed closely behind him.

Chapter Nineteen

He led me through the pack house, holding my hand tightly. We got to his Jeep and he opened the passenger side door for me. "After you."

I giggled a bit. "My, my. And they say chivalry is dead." He nudged my shoulder playfully. "I'm nothing if not a gentleman. Is that okay with you?" I could see that he was worried about my opinions and perception of him. I knew he wasn't trying to come off too strong. It was cute how hard he was trying just for him to turn around and get bashful.

I decided to tease him a bit. "Gentle… Sure." I climbed into the Jeep and buckled in. "You don't have to check in with me all the time, if I don't like something then trust that I'll say something. I expect you to do the same with me." I shut the door to the passenger side as he walked around the Jeep.

He laughed as he got into the driver's seat, buckling himself in. He turned and looked at me. "Fair enough, but I do have to make sure you're comfortable and feel safe at all times." He started the car and pulled out of the garage, starting to drive toward wherever he was taking me. "Can I ask you something?"

I smirked and looked at him. "You just did." I chuckled, smiling shyly.

He laughed a bit before speaking again. "I did, didn't I? Alright… let me rephrase then. Can I ask you another question?"

I wanted to keep teasing him, but he seemed like he had something important he wanted to talk about. "Sure." He glanced over at me before returning his eyes to the road.

He gathered his thoughts, it looked like this was really bothering him.

"Grey, what is it?"

It took a few seconds for him to speak. "Do you… do you trust me? And I'm not talking about just right now… I mean do you trust me in general?"

I furrowed my eyebrows and adjusted in my seat to face him a little more. "Where is this coming from?"

He kept his gaze on the road, he didn't want to meet my gaze. "I just… I just need to know if you trust me." Whatever was bothering him was obviously weighing on him, I could feel it as if it was my own stress. "Can you please answer the question?" He glanced at me, worry written all over his face.

I placed my hand on his leg, squeezing softly. "Of course I trust you. Why are you so worried about that?" I did my best to keep my tone calm, even though I was worried about him.

I could feel part of his tension release as I left my hand on his leg. "I don't know… I just feel like you don't trust me fully." He sighed and gripped the steering wheel tighter. "It's just… I feel like I have to earn your trust…"

I nodded and looked out the window, leaving my hand on his leg, wanting to offer him comfort even if it was a small gesture. "Trust is a constant state of proving you're worthy of it. I understand your concern, but I do trust you." I wanted to hug him, but he was driving and I didn't want to throw off his concentration. I hated seeing him so upset.

He placed one of his hands over mine, keeping the other hand firm on the steering wheel. "I appreciate that. I'm just worried that you'll never fully trust me."

I could feel how much this was bothering him, it bothered me too because he was right. I needed to be honest. "You're right, I won't" I closed my eyes, feeling a rush of anger and sadness. "It isn't your fault, please know that. My parents… my old pack… They ruined that for me. I trust you, I do. Maybe not fully, but I do, more than I've ever trusted anyone." I opened my eyes and turned my head away, looking out the window as the trees flew by. I couldn't look at his reaction, I didn't want to be the cause of any of his pain.

I could feel his heart break and I wish I couldn't. I wanted to be free with him, free to be at my most vulnerable. "Little one… I'm so sorry… I wish things could have been different for you. You don't have to fully trust me yet… I understand how hard it is." The car turned down a different road.

I sighed and kept looking out the window, trying to push down my emotions. I felt like I was going to crack at any second. "I'm sorry…" I wasn't even sure my voice was loud enough to be heard. I felt so small like I had done something wrong.

He let out a deep breath and pulled the Jeep over to the side of the road, turning off the engine and turning to look at me. "Look at me, please." I did as he asked, swallowing the lump forming in my throat. "You don't need to be sorry for anything…" He continued, I was feeling his heartbreak as he looked into my eyes. "I shouldn't have pressured you into answering my question… I'm sorry."

The car went silent for a moment, and the only sound that could be heard was our breathing. I stared out the window again, feeling the weight of my emotions. I closed my eyes and shook my head, my eyes returning to look at him as much as I couldn't take hurting him.

"You didn't pressure me to answer, I needed to be honest. I'm sorry that what I'm going through is affecting you. The last thing I want is to hurt you because I can't move on from my past." I let out a breath I hadn't realized I was holding and looked back down at my hands.

I felt so much weight on me, the number one pressure was not wanting to disappoint him.

He reached out and gently held my face in his hand. "Little one, it's okay…" I leaned into his touch, still fighting back against breaking. "You don't have to move on from your past right now… You just need time." He ran his thumb over my cheekbone. "If anything, I'm glad that you're being honest with me… It makes me feel like you trust me enough to open up about your past."

I looked up at him, I knew what I needed to do. I wasn't sure I was ready,that I'd ever be, but I had to be.

"Memory sharing… I want to show you the nightmare I keep having, my lowest point. It… It isn't pretty. It haunts me, but it's where my faith in anyone ever loving me broke." I looked down at my hands again, feeling unsure about this but knowing I had to.

He cupped my chin, making me look at him again. "Little one, you don't have to show me if you aren't ready." He was giving me a choice to back out but I knew I couldn't. "But… If you feel that you are ready, I want to help you through it."

I choked back my tears. "If I can't trust you fully, then I at least owe it to you to show you why." I closed my eyes and took a deep breath before opening them again. He was worried for me and I could see it as much as I could feel it.

"How do I show you? I'm ready." I wasn't but it was time I did this. No more hiding from my pain.

He leaned forward and wiped away the tears I didn't know escaped me. He nodded and leaned back in his seat, giving me a minute to regain my composure. "Just relax… take a deep breath and close your eyes."

I did as he told me to and rested against my seat. "I'll take you through your nightmare as best I can… you just need to focus on my voice and let me guide you through it."

I nodded and looked over at him. "Grey, if I start having a panic attack, please don't let me get in my head. That's where things get dark, and I don't know if I can handle that." He nodded as he met my gaze. "I won't let you get in your head... I promise." We both settled in our seats.

He took my hand in his and held it gently as he continued. "Now, close your eyes and focus on my voice. If you start feeling overwhelmed or like things are getting too dark for you to handle, just tell me and I'll bring you back. Are you ready?" I nodded and I tried to focus on his voice, breathing deeply and slowly. I closed my eyes and let the scene unfold in my head.

He took a deep breath and began to guide me through the nightmare, speaking gently and trying to keep me grounded in the present moment. "You're safe... you're here with me. You're in control of your thoughts and your emotions. Just focus on me, okay? Just listen to my voice." He paused for a moment, wanting to make sure that I was still there with him. "Can you see anything yet?" he asked softly, wanting to know if I had started to remember the dream or if he needed to give me more time.

There I was, completely immersed in the nightmare again. I was tied to the tree by my wrists, my back stripped bare. My father was yelling all sorts of vicious things at me, but I couldn't hear a single word. His whip came down against my back, breaking and shredding my skin. The sound of the whip cracking in the air, the echo weaving through the trees. Every time the whip made contact I screamed out no matter how much I tried to hold it in.

I could feel Greyson squeeze my hand. "It's okay… You're not there anymore… You're here with me. I'm right here." I tried to hold onto his voice.

The whip cracked against my back, one, two, three, it was relentless. My blood running down my shredded skin.

"Focus on me… focus on my voice. You're safe now… you can let go of your pain." His voice was a calm in the storm, but my father's relentless lashing was overwhelming.

I could feel my mind slipping into the nightmare, the feeling of the whip against my back, the tree I was wrapped around, the pain, the emotion of reminding myself why I was enduring this punishment.

I felt him tighten his grip on my hand again. "Little one… You're here with me, you're safe now."

My eyes darted open and I jumped forward with a start. My tears fell freely as I tried to catch my breath. I was shaking and crying, I was a mess. I felt my panic starting to rise and I tried to push it down.

He wrapped his arms around me and held me tightly against him. "It's okay… you're okay, you're safe now." I was shaking and couldn't stop. "Take deep breaths… slowly in… and out…" I did my best to follow his guidance. "That's it. You can do this little one. You just need a few moments to catch your breath and let everything out. Take as much time as you need."

My breaths came out in short gasps, but I slowly regained my composure. He held me tightly, letting me lean on him, and giving me time to steady myself. I slowly tried to steady my breathing, trying to focus on his voice and the feel of his arms around me.

He rubbed my back. "Just take it slow… I got you, you can do this. I'm right here." I calmed down enough to sit up on my own. I wiped my tears and took a shaky breath. He gave me a minute to collect myself. "You okay? Do you want to talk about it?" I leaned back against the seat and took another breath as I nodded, my tears still falling.

It took me a few minutes to find the right words, I felt so vulnerable and broken. Reliving that moment always made me feel like my father was right and I had no worth.

"I don't trust, not because people don't earn it. I give my trust in abundance, I've trusted blindly my whole life… I trusted my parents, and it's a thing that every girl's first love is their father." I took another shaky breath. "A girl is supposed to feel safe and protected when it comes to their father. He… Alexander… proved time and time again that I would never find that in him." I leaned my head back and closed my eyes, my tears still falling. I didn't fight them.

"I'm sorry… No one should ever have to go through what you did." I could feel his concern, his wanting to comfort me. "Did you ever tell anyone what Alexander did to you?"

I shook my head without hesitation. "That's what makes it worse… The whole pack knew they saw how he'd treat me, and they'd just turn a blind eye to it. I trusted my entire pack and they abandoned me to the abuse I faced every day. It wasn't just Alexander who broke my trust, it was everyone." I looked over at him.

His eyes searched mine like he was pleading to let him hold me. "That's so unfair… No one should ever have to face abuse, especially not from their own family." His face softened as he continued to keep eye contact with me. "How are you feeling now?"

I took a sharp breath in and turned away from him as I looked out the windshield. "I think I'll be okay. I'm a bit shaken but I'm okay." I couldn't tell if I was lying. Honestly… I felt numb.

He took my hand in his again and squeezed lightly. "You can take as much time as you need… Just know that I'm here for you." He took a minute holding my hand before speaking again. "Do you want me to drive back to the pack's compound?" Although his voice was kind, it was laced with concern.

"No." I looked back over at him, offering a small smile. "Let's keep going, I want to see your safe place."

He smiled back at me, but he couldn't hide the worry in his eyes. "Okay… Let's keep going." He turned the Jeep back on and put it back in drive. "We should be there soon… We're just getting onto the main road." He glanced over at me. "Do you need anything else right now?"

I chuckled and looked down at my hands as I sniffled. "No, I'm okay." I thought for a moment. "How about some music? I have to warn you though, my playlist can get pretty sad… ugh, but the songs are so good." I looked back over at him, smiling genuinely.

It felt good to share that with him, like one less thing I have to go through alone.

"Music sounds nice… How about starting with something upbeat?"

I laughed and looked through the songs on my phone. "I make no promises my love." I paused my scrolling and immediately started blushing realizing the words that just rolled off my tongue. I cleared my throat and started scrolling again until I found something upbeat and started connecting my phone to the car. I could feel his eyes on me and tried to shake the feeling as I struggled to connect my phone.

"Your love?" His voice was curious and teasing. I started the song and sat back in my seat trying to ignore the question. He recognized the song almost instantly and started to sing along with it. "Oh, I love this song!" He was so excited.

"So you sing too?!" I was snapped from my embarrassment completely. "Grey, what else should I know? Because I swear you get more and more perfect with every passing moment." I could feel myself blushing again as I looked at him.

He laughed and kept his eyes on the road, glancing over at me occasionally. "Yeah, I can sing… but I don't think anyone would want to hear me. And I'm far from perfect…" He kept singing with what was playing before speaking again. "What about you? Do you have any special skills or talents?"

I shook my head. "Oh no, no, no. You are not getting out of this. Prepare for the biggest ego boost of your life." I cleared my throat and lowered the volume to the music just barely loud enough to hear. I sat up straight in my seat and turned slightly to look at him.

He got comfortable in his seat and glanced over at me for a second. "Oh? Are you about to tell me how amazing I am?"

I wanted to wipe that arrogant smirk off of his face but I remained in my seat and didn't hit him although it would've been satisfying. "You want to kill the moment?" I smirked, raising an eyebrow.

He shook his head and laughed. "No, no… I'm just enjoying how confident you are right now." He cleared his throat and kept his eyes on the road. "I appreciate your honesty… and your confidence is actually quite attractive." His smirk faded into a smile.

"Okay, okay. I'm supposed to be complimenting you here." I fake pouted as I spoke.

He laughed again. "Okay then… Go ahead, you have one chance." He was practically grinning from ear to ear.

The song came to an end and the next song started playing, something much slower and more romantic than the previous one. "Well, if that wasn't perfect timing." He laughed, the tension slowly easing.

I took a breath. "Greyson Carver, alpha of the Wind Walker pack. You are single-handedly the most infuriating person I have ever met… but…" I took another breath and this time looked directly at him. "You are also the most caring. There is no one I'd rather have as my mate."

The car jerked for a moment then continued moving. Greyson was stunned for a minute. "Wait… What did you just say? Did I hear you right?" He had the biggest smile on his face.

I spilled my feelings without thinking twice about it. "We've already marked each other. The entire pack knows about us… I think… I think I've always felt this way, I just didn't know how to express it out of fear."

He kept driving, but the smile on his face kept growing more genuine by the second. "And your fears are perfectly valid little one."

I placed my hand on his leg, squeezing lightly. "I appreciate everything you've done for me, not one thing has gone unnoticed."

He placed his hand over mine. "You've always felt this way? Are you sure? I mean… I feel the same way about you… but I don't want to assume anything."

I giggled and moved my hand to my mouth trying not to laugh too hard. "My love, you're rambling again."

He couldn't help but laugh. "Sorry… I just wasn't expecting to hear this from you right now." He gripped the steering wheel again and adjusted himself in his seat. "You don't know how long I've wanted to tell you how I feel… but I didn't want to risk ruining what we had."

I raised the volume of the music. "Okay, okay. Enough being sappy until we get to wherever you're taking me." I laughed and then started singing along to what was playing.

As we continued driving, I looked around admiring the interior of the Jeep and the passing scenery as I continued singing along to the music. Greyson sang along then and there, keeping his eyes on the road. "You know… I think this is probably one of my favorite drives ever." As we continued driving, I looked over at him and smiled. He was beautiful, and the way he looked at me made my heart flutter. I wanted to tell him how I felt, but I was afraid of him rejecting me. "Hey… Can I ask you something?" His question snapped me from my thoughts. I looked back at him and nodded. I was a bit concerned he wasn't happy. "How long have you felt this way about me?"

I looked back out at the road as he drove. "Since we met. The day you found me in the woods… I knew I was supposed to be with you, I knew I was going to fall for you, and… It petrified me. I was worried this was going to turn out like it had growing up, that you and the pack would reject me like my parents did."

He gripped the steering wheel tighter, I couldn't tell if it was anger or frustration. "Why didn't you tell me sooner? I mean… I can't imagine what you must have been going through all this time."

I took a breath. The truth? I didn't know why I didn't say anything. "Well, I was struggling to come to terms with that being how I felt… Then the argument we had about that day I followed you into the woods didn't exactly help me with expressing it. In truth, you were right. I wanted people to view me as the helpless pup, but that's because that's how I felt… Small and helpless."

He took my hand in his and kissed it while keeping his eyes on the road. "I get it… you want people to see you as a leader, not a pup… But don't ever feel like you have to be someone you're not around me… I already think you're pretty amazing," he said with a smile.

The sun was setting in the sky, casting a beautiful glow over the landscape as we drove through the countryside. The music was uplifting and I felt my worries melt away as we spent time together. The road became steep and windy as we climbed higher and higher into the mountains, and I could feel the thrill of adventure in my heart.

He glanced over at me with a childlike smile, he couldn't contain his excitement. "You know… I have a surprise for you. It's kind of a big deal, so I want you to close your eyes while I drive." I looked at him with a confused smile, I complied nonetheless, covered my eyes, and rested my head against the seat.

"Does that mean we're almost there?" I could hear him laugh slightly.

"Yes… we're almost there." I didn't need to see to know how happy he was.

Chapter Twenty

We drove for a few more minutes and then the Jeep stopped. "Okay… you can open your eyes now."

When I opened my eyes there was a cabin, it looked like it was built personally. There was a porch swing and a firepit. "Grey… where are we?" I continued taking in my surroundings.

"We're at my family's cabin." He took in his surroundings as well, a look of calm and satisfaction on his face. "I know it's not much, but I wanted to share it with you."

As I continued looking at the cabin from the car, I felt my heart swelling with so much love for him. He never spoke about his family. Rather than sharing his memories with me, he brought me here to show it to me. I couldn't put how I was feeling into words, I could only hope our mate bond would tell him, that he'd feel it with me, for me.

He turned off the car and stepped out of it. "Come on… I have something else I want to show you." I took a breath so I wouldn't make a fool of myself, but I was so excited it was hard to contain. I undid the buckle to my seatbelt and took my time getting out of the Jeep so I wouldn't fall again. He laughed as he watched me getting out of the Jeep. "Here, let me help you." He closed the driver's side door, walked around the Jeep, and extended his hand to me. I took his hand and he helped steady myself as I stood up. "You alright?"

I nodded and looked up at him, still holding his hands. "A bit sore from falling earlier but I'll survive."

He smiled and squeezed my hands. "Well, at least you didn't get hurt too badly." He let go of my hands and started walking towards the cabin. "Come on… I'll give you a full tour."

I ran up to him and held his arm with both hands. "What are you showing me first?" I felt like a kid in a candy store.

He looked at me and smiled as we walked together. "Well, I want to take you inside first so you can see my favorite place in the house." We continued walking towards the door. "Trust me… you're going to love this." I could tell he was just as excited to show me everything as much as I was excited to see it all.

He opened the door and led me inside. I walked in, looking around wide-eyed at the cabin's interior. "I know it's not much… but it's home to me." He looked around with a heavy heart and a small bit of nostalgia. "What do you think?"

I looked around, taking in the cozy atmosphere and the smell of the wood that held the structure of the cabin together. "It's perfect… I love it."

He took a few steps deeper into the cabin and opened a door, leading me into his favorite room. "This is my favorite part of the house…" He gestured for me to come into the room with him.

I stepped inside the room and my jaw dropped. "A personal library?" The smell of books new and old filled the room. There was a large oak desk that looked hand-crafted right by the window. "Was this your father's den?"

I looked over at Greyson, who looked deep in thought. He walked over to the oak desk and sat down, looking over at me with a grin. "Yeah, this was my father's study. He used to spend hours in here reading and writing. I would come in here all the time to bother him… but I guess I never thought about how special it would become for me." He looked down at the desk, running his hand over the wood.

I walked over to the window and looked out over the snow-covered trees. It was a beautiful sight and I felt so content here. He got up from the desk and walked over to me. He stood behind me and wrapped his arms around my waist, holding me close to him.

"I love how peaceful it is here." I leaned my head back against him and admired the white blankets of snow canvasing over the landscape. "I can see why this place is your escape." I sighed feeling lighter than I have in a long time.

"I've always come here when I need a break from everything else in my life… I feel like I can forget about all my worries here." He held me closer and rested his chin against my shoulder. "I hope you feel the same way…"

I wrapped my arm up and around his neck and ran my fingers through his hair as I left my head resting against him. "Thank you for sharing this with me."

He hugged me tighter. "You're welcome… I just wanted to share it with you. You can come here anytime you want… we can always come here together."

I nodded and looked up at him. "I don't think I could get here on my own even if I wanted to." I laughed a bit. "For one, I can't drive… and it wouldn't feel right. It's beautiful and peaceful and I can see myself enjoying being here… but this isn't my space and being here alone would feel like I'm intruding."

He laughed with me and nodded in agreement. "I know what you mean... it's kind of a special place for me, so I would want you to be here with me if that makes sense," he said softly, wanting me to feel like I belonged here. "I know it's not much... but it's my home and you're always welcome here. No matter what happens between us, this place will always have a special place in my heart and I want you to be part of it."

I melted at his words and I smiled softly. "I love you Greyson."

He smiled down at me and leaned down, capturing my lips in a soft tender kiss. "I love you too little one… more than anything in this world." He kissed me again and pulled away after a few seconds. "I know we have a lot to figure out between us… but I hope you know that I will never give up on us."

I giggled slightly. "I'm going to hold you to that."

He smiled and kissed my cheek. "I'm serious… I don't ever want to lose you." He let me go and took a few steps back, looking around the room once again. I could tell he had a lot on his mind. "We should go back outside… It's a beautiful day out there."

I ran up and grabbed his arm again. "Okay." I started to feel a little hot but I ignored it since I shouldn't be in heat this soon.

We started walking toward the door but he stopped and looked at me worried. "Are you alright? You're looking a bit flushed." I furrowed my eyebrows as he looked at me like he was studying me. "Are you… feeling alright?"

I tilted my head and shrugged. "I feel okay, a little warm but I'm okay."

He sighed and shook his head. "Are you sure? It's alright if you're in heat."

I felt my face heat up, I knew I was blushing. "I… I shouldn't be. I'll admit I feel a bit hot but I think I'm okay." I couldn't tell who I was trying to convince.

"You're not feeling any other symptoms of heat?" He pulled away from me and took a step back. "Maybe I should give you some space…" I felt a bit sad that he stepped away from me, but I understood why he did. I could feel a subtle rise in my body temperature but paid it no mind. "I think you should get some rest… I know being in heat can be really tiring." I knew what he was doing, which only made me feel worse.

I just wanted to enjoy being here with him. I nodded and lowered my head. He gave me a quick kiss on my cheek then walked away from me heading toward the front door.

"I'm sorry… I just don't want to make you feel uncomfortable." He reached for the door. "Call me if you need anything… I'll be outside."

He left the cabin and as the door opened his scent carried in the air causing the heat in my body to rise faster. I stayed quiet, feeling a bit hurt but understanding. I sat down on the couch and stared out the window, trying to forget about the heat and the tension in the room.

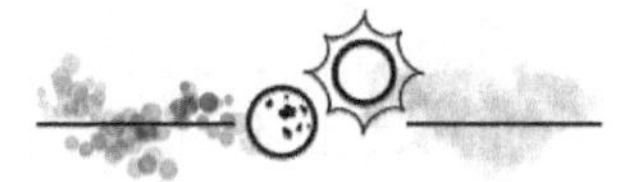

Chapter Twenty-One

I sat on the couch for a while, feeling the heat intensify. I tried to distract myself by thinking about the scenery outside the window but I found it difficult to focus.

Eventually, I fell asleep, hoping that the rest would help me clear my mind. As I slept I found myself reliving the same nightmare as my body temperature continued to rise. The whip came down against my bare back in the memory and my body temperature continued rising in reality. Both sensations were unbearable but I couldn't shake either one.

"Little one… sweetheart, wake up. Please…" I heard him. He shook me gently, his touch snapping me from my subconscious and sending a tidal wave of heat through me simultaneously.

I sat up panicked and overwhelmed physically. "It's okay… it was just a dream. Are you okay?" I took a deep breath and swallowed hard trying to control myself. I shook my head desperately trying to keep my composure but the level of heat I was experiencing was enough to make any sane person crack mentally. "It's okay… deep breaths." He gave me a moment to try and calm down but the heat was becoming more noticeable. "Come on little one… let me help you."

I shook my head and stood sitting on the couch. I put my head in my hands still trying to keep control over myself. "I don't want to force you to take me to bed every time I get like this."

He walked in front of me. "You don't have to force me… I want to take care of you." He kneeled in front of me so I could look at him. "Please… let me help you little one. I know how much this heat can affect you." His voice was soft and sincere.

"I don't want it to be like this every time!" A low growl escaped me as I spoke and I could feel my eyes glowing softly. "I… I don't want to be a burden to you. I know how much I am already."

He shook his head. "You're not a burden… you're my little one and I love taking care of you. This is just what happens when you go into heat… there's nothing we can do to change it."

I shut my eyes tightly as I felt my body temperature start rising again, his scent lingering in the air making it harder to control myself. "I don't know how much longer I can stay in control." My hands gripped my hair trying to focus on anything other than my heat.

"Just relax… you don't have to stay in control right now. Just let yourself go, let yourself feel it… let me take care of you." He stood knelt in front of me. I opened my eyes, they were still glowing. The golden color reflected off of him.

"Do you even understand what you're asking?" My body temperature spiked causing me to bite my lip before I could scream as I doubled over, still sitting on the couch.

"I understand exactly what I'm asking." He held his hand out toward me. "Let me help you… let me take care of you." I took his hand and my heat immediately got worse, I squeezed his hand and bit back another scream. I could feel tears running down my face as I did my best to fight back against everything I was feeling. "Let go… let it take over…" He squeezed my hand back. "Let yourself feel the pleasure, let me take care of you."

I nodded hesitantly. I allowed him to help me up but every time he touched me, my body temperature would rise that much more.

He got me as far as the hallway before I couldn't keep control anymore. My wolf took over completely and there was nothing I could do about it. I slammed him against the wall and kissed him hungrily. He let me take complete control over him, returning the kiss with just as much hunger as I felt. "Do what you need to do." His lips crashed against mine. "I'm yours." His hands made their way to my face, holding me tightly in place. "Take me." His voice was pleading but drenched in desire. "Take me now." His hands came down to the neck of my shirt and tore it open, the rush of cool air against my skin sent me through the roof with desire.

I could feel his heart pounding as my body arched into his. Our kiss grew more passionate every second we remained locked together. He pushed my shirt off of my shoulders, letting it fall to the floor before his hands gripped my waist pulling me as close to him as I could get.

I broke the kiss for a moment, pulling his shirt over his head not wanting to waste a second. He kissed me briefly before his lips started to travel from my lips down my jawline, continuing down my neck. He was nipping and licking the most sensitive parts of my neck making me moan out. I couldn't think of anything other than him.

I slammed him back against the wall and kissed him again as my hands started untying the drawstring to his sweatpants. He didn't give me any time to pull his pants down before he lifted me up into his arms, his hands gripping my ass as he carried me to his bed.

He threw me on the bed and flipped me over his hands, finding the seam of my pants and tearing them open completely. I hadn't had on any panties since falling earlier in the day left me in more pain with any unnecessary pressure applied.

He groaned at the sight of how wet I was. He pulled away for a moment. "Don't move an inch." His voice was commanding and full of lust. I obeyed, not moving a muscle in any direction. He pulled his sweatpants and boxers down then climbed onto the bed behind me. He gripped my hips, pulling me up onto all fours. He moved one hand to my neck, snaking it around and squeezing my throat. He groaned in my ear holding me in place as he kissed my shoulder leaving a trail of fire.

He slammed me back down against the bed leaving my legs propping my ass up for him. "Now are you gonna be a good girl for me?" I nodded, moving my legs around him. "That's my good girl, but that's not how I want you." He climbed off the bed and came back, flipping me onto my back.

Before I could react he tied my wrists together and restrained me to the headboard. I wasn't afraid, every nerve in my body was screaming for him. "Now, the only thing you have to do is enjoy the way I'm about to take you like the little slut you know you are."

Although his words were demeaning, I loved every second of it. I nodded my head and he towered over me. He tore my legs apart and bent my knees. He pressed himself against me and kissed my chest as his hand came down between my legs. His finger teased every fold and sensitive bit of my already-drenched cunt.

"Good girl, you're already dripping at the mere thought of me." I moaned as his fingers continued to work over my clit.

His groans turned into low guttural growls as he slid inside of me. "You're so fucking tight." My head tilted back as my moans became more frequent. I tugged against the restraints as his every move against me made me crave more. "What's wrong little one?" His tone was teasing in every sense of the word.

I couldn't speak, all that came out was moans. I was a mess. I could feel myself dripping.

He started to pound into me with an animalistic force. I wrapped my legs around his waist. "Now, now little one…" He gripped my hips, his thumbs digging in making me let him go. He leaned down and whispered in my ear as his hand wrapped around my throat, "Right now, you're my slut… I'm in charge." He pounded into me even harder, the bedframe banging against the wall.

"G-Grey…" I couldn't form a coherent sentence, I was completely lost in the pure passion of the moment.

My thoughts were as scrambled as my insides were going to be by the time he was done with me. He pulled out of me and flipped me over, the restraints tightening as they twisted.

He slammed back into me making my back arch and a whimper escaping me. His hands held my hips, tightening his grip with each thrust. The sound of our skin smacking together and our moans echoing through the room, spilling into the rest of the cabin.

I couldn't hold back anymore. I bit my lip as my body started tensing up and a knot twisted in my stomach.

"Let go little one, I want to hear you enjoying yourself."

On command I let go of my tension, surrendering to him as my moans got louder, I could feel myself tightening around him which only made me feel him pounding into me that much more. I could feel him tense up inside of me.

"Fuck, you feel so good." He pounded into me with a force I didn't know he was capable of.

With one final thrust into me, I could feel him let go. He didn't stop but he slowed down his pace, a warmth spreading in me as he made sure he spilled into me completely, careful not to let a single drop of him go to waste.

He pulled out and let the restraints loose and I collapsed against the bed. I was spent but completely satisfied as the heat in my body receded to the point my temperature regulated.

Greyson lay down next to me still breathing heavily. "How do you feel?"

I couldn't bring myself to speak so I simply nodded. I stood lying down on my stomach but turned my head to look at him.

He looked exhausted. He reached his hand out and ran his fingers through my hair gently. "Are you okay?"

I nodded again. "Thank you…" My words were breathy, I wasn't too sure my voice was even audible.

"You're welcome little one… It's my pleasure to take care of you." He continued stroking my hair. "Take your time… rest." I could tell he was still worried about me.

My eyes fluttered shut, the exhaustion I was feeling was taking over.

"Rest now, you don't have to worry about anything right now other than you." He kissed my forehead and I melted further into sleep. "Sleep well… I'll be here when you wake up."

Chapter Twenty-Two

When I woke up I was sore and disoriented, I took a moment to look around. I was in Greyson's arms and he was still fast asleep. I smiled softly and nuzzled into him letting out a contented sigh. I watched his eyes start to open and I felt a little bad for waking him up. He smiled down at me, still half asleep.

"How do you feel, little one?" His voice sent shivers down my spine, he was still so tired.

"Better a little sore but better, thank you for taking care of me even though I was being stubborn." I hugged him tighter, enjoying how warm he was.

He wrapped his arms around me tighter. "You're welcome. Just know that you don't have to be afraid to give in to your desires… I love taking care of you and I don't mind if you get a bit possessive." Even as tired as he was, he was still teasing me.

I brought my head down between my shoulders, sinking into myself, suddenly remembering slamming him into the wall. "I'm sorry, I didn't hurt you, did I?"

He chuckled at my reaction. "Don't worry… you didn't hurt me. It was just a bit of rough play… I've had worse." He winked at me. His playful attempt didn't go unnoticed but I knew that the 'worse' he experienced wasn't with me. I snuggled closer to him feeling a bit cold. "Are you feeling a bit cold? Do you want me to get you a blanket?"

I shivered slightly and nodded. "I wouldn't need a blanket if someone didn't tear my clothes."

He got up from the bed and kissed my forehead. "I'm sorry… I got a bit carried away. Let me go get you something warm…" He left the room and came back with a blanket. "Here you go little one." He handed me the blanket and sat back down on the bed. He opened the blanket and tucked it around me. I already felt warmer.

I looked out the window to see that it was snowing. "Looks like we won't be making it back to the pack house for a while."

He looked out the window. "I guess not… It looks like we're stuck here for a bit. It could be worse." He chuckled and I joined in.

I looked up at him and smiled. "There's no one else I'd rather be stranded with."

He smiled down at me and caressed my cheek. "I feel the same way little one, I don't mind being stranded with you… as long as we're together." He kissed my forehead again and guided my head to rest on his chest.

We spent a few hours in bed cuddled up while the snow continued falling outside. "Hey, Grey?"

He had an arm wrapped around me and opened an eye when he heard my voice. "Yes, little one? What is it?"

I suddenly felt a bit nervous and looked down, my hand resting on his chest while my fingers traced his tattoos. "Neither of us have eaten and it's already pretty late."

His hand rubbed my shoulder easing my nerves. "I didn't even realize how late it was… we've been in bed together for a few hours." He looked out the window, holding me tighter. "Yeah, I guess we should probably eat something… I'm starting to get hungry." He chuckled.

I looked up at him, my gaze locked with his. "We can't stay here forever Grey." I felt a twinge of sadness at the thought of leaving our little paradise.

"I know… I don't want to leave either. We can enjoy it while we're here though." He kissed my forehead leaving his hand on my face. "It'll be okay… we'll find our way back to the pack soon enough." He smiled at me but I still felt sad about the idea of leaving.

"What if… what if we stood the weekend? I'm sure the pack can survive without us for a couple of days…" I smiled up at him hopeful he'd agree, but knowing there was a higher chance of us staying not being likely.

"I… I don't know if we can do that little one." He brushed some of the hair away from my face. "I want to stay here as much as you do, but we have responsibilities back at the pack house. We can't just abandon our duties for an entire weekend." I looked away from him, my heart sinking.

I felt like crying, but I tried to hold back tears. "Hey, little one… don't be sad. We'll come back here again soon, I promise." He held me closer against him. I looked up at him, my eyes still filled with tears.

I wanted to believe him, but the reality of the situation was starting to set in. "How is it, even when you pick to be with me… being alpha always comes first?" I sat up and looked away from him, wiping my stray tears away. "What happened to delegating and sharing the weight of our responsibilities with the betas?" I held myself, refusing to look back at him.

"Look at me little one." I hesitated but obeyed. "I can't just leave everything behind… I have responsibilities as the alpha of my pack. It's not fair to them if I just disappear for a weekend."

I shook my head and looked away from him again. "Our… our pack, our responsibilities." I paused for a moment trying to think everything through. I stood up from the bed and wrapped the blanket around me tightly. "I think I'm going to sleep on the couch until the blizzard passes." I didn't look back at him, I just walked out of the room and sat on the couch. I could still hear him from the bedroom.

"Little one… please, come back to bed." I didn't move from the couch. I picked up my phone and started dialing Shade. "Don't be mad at me… I just have to do my job." I clicked the call button.

It didn't take long for Shade to pick up. "Hey Luna, what's up?"

I took a breath and pinched the bridge of my nose. "Hey Shade, how's the pack holding up with the blizzard?"

She giggled at my tone, I swear I love this girl, she gets me. "Trouble in paradise? No, the pack is fine."

I let out a breath. "Do you think you guys would be okay without me and Greyson for the weekend?" I knew pushing this would make him angry but I just wanted to spend time with him without worrying.

"Yeah, I think we can manage. Just keep your phone close just in case." She seemed like she was thinking about something.

"Shade? What's going on in that head of yours? I know what your voice sounds like when you start planning something."

She laughed but didn't answer my question. "Just enjoy your weekend." And with that, she hung up without another word. I sighed and tossed my phone on the couch.

I sat alone on the couch for a while, I didn't want to go back to bed just to argue again. "Do you want me to leave you alone?" I couldn't tell his choice of tone and sighed.

"I'd prefer you not make me feel like my opinion doesn't matter," I shouted back so he could hear me from this distance.

"I know you have an opinion… and I care about your feelings, but I also have a responsibility to the pack… and I can't just leave them behind."

I leaned forward resting my head in my hands, choking my emotions back. "According to Shade everyone is fine and they'll continue to be if we took some time away for ourselves."

He was silent for a moment, the dead air killing me. "Well… I appreciate Shade's opinion, but I still can't just abandon my pack. I have a duty to protect them… and I can't just leave that behind for a weekend." His tone was firm like he was trying to assert his dominance.

"Two steps forward seven steps back." I shook my head and got up from the couch, walking back into the bedroom. "Clothes? I need some air." I didn't look at him, I couldn't.

"I have clothes you can borrow." He got up from the bed and dug through the dresser in the room. "You can go out for some air… but please don't be gone for too long." He handed me the clothes and I took them, putting them on. I turned around, put on my shoes, and grabbed his coat on the way out, not saying anything, just leaving.

The air outside was cold, it was hard to breathe easily with the wind blowing. I walked around for a while before finding a stump in the wooded area around the cabin. I sat on the stump and held my head in my hands. I took down the braid Greyson had done for me earlier in the day and feathered my hair out.

I have no idea how long I was gone, but I couldn't be in the same room as him right now. His words weren't what hurt... It was that despite all the talking and all the planning to help him have a clearer schedule so we can spend time together and so he wouldn't be so stressed, he was still picking the pack over everything else. It wasn't just my opinion that didn't matter... I didn't matter.

Greyson Carver, my mate, alpha of the Wind Walker pack. His favorite flower, lilies. Favorite food, steak, specifically rib eye. Not picky when it comes to music and enjoys reading as long as the plot can attract his attention. His favorite color is every hue of blue the skies and bodies of water can produce. He has two siblings, the twins, Teagan and Tristan. They lost their parents at a young age, murder, and the twins were present for it and survived.

Greyson is the most stubborn yet kind-hearted man I've ever met. He strives on his honor and commitments to his pack and that is admirable. What I don't understand is, how can he be so all in with being alpha but fail so miserably when it comes to his mate, me.

I had been so lost in thought I didn't realize the blizzard had picked up. My lap was covered in at least six inches of snow. I wasn't ready to go back inside. It was becoming hazardous to stay where I was. I made my way back to the cabin and sat on the stairs leading to the porch. The cold numbed my skin, but his choices numbed me, mind, body, and soul.

I heard the door open but I didn't turn around. "Little one... you shouldn't have been out there for so long. Why don't you come back inside? You could get sick... or worse." I didn't say anything, I didn't turn to look at him, I just sat there. He walked over and crouched down next to me. "Little one... can you please look at me? I just want to make sure you're okay." I didn't look at him.

"Go back inside, it's cold and you're wearing sweatpants and a t-shirt." He seemed shocked by my reaction, I don't know what he expected.

"Little one... I don't care about the cold right now, I just want to make sure that alright. Please come back inside with me..." I went back to not speaking. I leaned forward slightly, resting my elbows on my knees and holding myself.

He spent a while trying to get me inside, begging, pleading. I didn't respond, I didn't move. "Little one... please..." I couldn't take his begging anymore. I stood up and went inside, hanging up his coat and kicking off my shoes.

I walked into the bathroom, locked the door, and started the shower. He knocked on the door as I started to take off the snow-soaked clothes I was wearing. "Little one? Can we talk about this?" I didn't respond. I put the clothes I was wearing on the counter and got into the shower. "I don't want to leave things like this. Can we just talk about what happened earlier?" I didn't respond. I just stood there silently, letting the hot water run over my body. He knocked again, softer this time. "Little one... please..." I held my breath and let the water run down my hair and over my face.

He didn't stop pleading through the door. I finished my shower, turned off the water and wrapped a towel around myself leaving my hair down, dripping. I opened the door, still not looking at him. "Little one... let's talk about earlier. I know that I hurt your feelings... but I can't just abandon my responsibilities as alpha."

As he spoke I could feel my anger rising. I finally looked up at him, a low growl coming from me. "I am only going to say this once. I admire your concern for the pack, but your responsibilities are mine too. I'd choose you over the pack any day at the drop of a pin. Without you, there is no pack. As much as you have a responsibility to them you have a responsibility to me, I'm your mate for fucks sake yet I always get the back burner."

He raised an eyebrow as my growl escaped me. "I understand where you're coming from... and I know that I haven't been fair to you. But you have to understand that I can't just abandon being the alpha. I care about you... but I can't just ignore my pack."

I pushed past him and walked into the room to grab clean clothes. "Get your priorities straight." I huffed as I passed him.

I started to grab clothes from his dresser. He walked in a few seconds after I did. "I'm sorry Naphinae. Can we please talk about this? I don't want us to fight..." I pulled his pants on and sighed. I couldn't take much more of this. I slipped his shirt over my head and looked at him as I pulled my hair out from under the shirt.

"There's nothing to talk about. You view taking a break as abandoning, even though you know the ranks of the pack hierarchy can handle your absence for a weekend you still choose to burden yourself." I paused for a moment to attempt to keep my composure. "Your head is so far up your own ass that you can't see that time and time again... you've abandoned me! And I am sick of being everyone's last concern..."

His face softened. "Little one..." He looked like he wanted to walk up to me and I put my hands up telling him to stop, he sighed and stood in place. "I know I've been unfair to you... and I can't begin to explain how sorry I am."

I shook my head and kept his gaze. "Save it. You can be sorry all you want, you're just going to keep doing it." I lowered my head, feeling defeated.

"I can't make excuses for what I did... but please believe me when I say that you mean everything to me." I couldn't bring myself to look at him anymore.

Before I could say anything, an arrow shot through the window and landed on the wall, the arrowhead implanting in the wall. Greyson rushed past me and straight up to the window. "Stay behind me... stay back." He stood between me and the window.

I was already angry and sinking my teeth into something just might be the thing to make me feel better. I approached the arrow that was embedded in the wall and pulled it out.

"Little one... please be careful." I looked at the arrow, and it looked like it had a purple powder on it. "Don't touch that! That's wolfsbane." He took the arrow from me.

"Wolfsbane?" I looked at him confused.

"Yes... it's a poison that can be deadly to werewolves," he said gently. "It was put on that arrow in order to hurt or kill anyone who might be hit by it." He threw the arrow on the ground, breaking it into pieces. "Good riddance," he said with a hint of disgust. "Little one, please don't go outside again. It's not safe."

I felt conflicted, I wanted to find out who did this. We wouldn't be safe here if they were still outside. I wanted to listen but I needed to figure this out with or without him. "I'll go investigate outside. Please, stay here where it's safe."

I laughed as I looked at him. "If you think I'm not going, then you're delusional." I started walking toward the front door, putting my shoes back on.

He followed me. "Little one… please, don't do this. I can handle this by myself… you don't need to put yourself in danger."

I stood up from tying my shoes and looked Greyson dead in the eyes. "You may be my alpha but you are my mate. That may not mean much to you… to me, that means we are in this together. Quit your whining and let's go." I opened the door and stepped outside.

He stepped outside behind me. "Naphinae… I'm sorry." I shook my head as I looked around for anything or anyone out of place. "This isn't the time and you know that." I walked down the front steps and could smell something sour in the air, it had to be more wolfsbane. "Grey?" I kept looking around trying to find the source of the smell. "Are the neighbors around us wolves too?"

He seemed worried. "Please don't get any closer. That could be more wolfsbane."

I turned to face him. "You didn't answer my question… Are the neighbors around us werewolves?"

He went pale. "Yes… some of them are."

I brought my hand up to my head trying to think. "Go warn them, I can handle this."

He nodded. "Okay… be careful." He ran off toward the other houses.

I turned my attention to the smell, following cautiously. As I walked further into the woods I saw someone, I approached slowly to observe them. It was a boy, he looked no older than 18. I got a little closer and a twig snapped under my shoe and I hid behind a tree.

"W-who's there?" He was looking around, he seemed afraid. He kept his crossbow aimed. I stood behind the tree and didn't risk moving into his sight, his scent reeked of wolfsbane. "I don't want to hurt you."

I took a breath. "What are you doing out here?"

I could hear him moving around trying to find me. "Uh, I was just walking around to get some exercise. W-what are you doing out here?" He was still moving.

I stood hidden. "Don't bullshit me, kid. Exercise doesn't require a crossbow."

He stopped moving, he knew I'd caught him. "Well, you see, uh… I was going hunting. Yeah, that's it." I could hear the nerves in his voice.

I took a step to get a better look at him but quickly withdrew once the snow crunched under my shoe. "Hunting huh? Hunting what?"

He hesitated for a moment before answering he then took a step back. "Uh, just some deer that I saw roaming in the forest." I couldn't see him but I knew he was loading his crossbow, the smell of wolfsbane was getting stronger.

"Is that why you reek of wolfsbane, kid?" He responded but I couldn't hear him, Greyson's scent taking over. Greyson was getting closer and fast. "If you know what's good for you then you'll leave." He started to approach me, I couldn't protect him if Greyson found him.

"W-what?! Why would I leave?" I could hear his crossbow in his hands, shaking slightly. Before I could say anything Greyson came barrelling toward the kid. "What the hell is that?!" I heard the kid raise his crossbow and I stepped in between them taking the hit for Greyson.

The arrow piercing through my shoulder hurt like hell, but the wolfsbane was as if someone left the arrowhead in close contact with an open flame. The kid ran off as I fell to the snow beneath me, the searing pain of the wolfsbane getting worse by the second.

Greyson rushed over to me. "Naphinae!" He knelt next to me, examining the wound. "You took the arrow for me." I could see the guilty look in his eyes. I clutched my bleeding shoulder, the arrow was embedded but not all the way through. I wasn't sure if I'd make it with the level of pain I was in.

He packed my shoulder with snow. "Stay with me… Just hold on… I'm going to get you out of here." He was pleading with me, he sounded desperate. He lifted me up and I did my best to hold onto him. He put me in the car and buckled me in the passenger seat.

My vision was blurring but I fought back with every ounce of strength I had remaining. He rushed around the Jeep and got into the driver's seat. "Don't leave me… please. I don't want to lose you… I can't." He started the car and drove off into the blizzard. Every bump in the road made me want to scream, the pain from my shoulder was radiating. I just hope he couldn't feel the pain I was through our bond. I didn't want him to know how much pain I was in.

He was speeding toward the pack house but we were pretty far, it was going to take an eternity to get back, especially with this blizzard. "Stay with me Naph, just hold on." He kept talking, pleading, trying to keep me awake. He pushed the Jeep to drive as fast as he could.

We made it back to the pack house, the car swerving to a stop. He left the Jeep running and got out coming over to the passenger side to get me out of the Jeep, he picked me up and carried me inside leaving the Jeep doors open. "Little one, just hang on." He carried me inside and brought me into a room, my vision was blurring, and I couldn't make out my surroundings. He laid me down on a bed and I felt a second set of hands on me but I couldn't hear anything.

I could feel myself fading.

Chapter Twenty-Three

-GREYSON-

I saw the way she was struggling to stay conscious and immediately started panicking. "Help! Someone please help me!" I couldn't lose her. The pack doctor came running in, I was shocked she was awake. Shade followed closely behind. "Please… help her." I stepped back and gave the doctor space to work trying to keep myself calm.

"Naphinae? No… Alpha what happened?" Shade whimpered at the sight of her injured luna, she seemed panicked.

I felt a wave of concern wash over me hearing shade whimper. "Shade… I'm so sorry. We— We were attacked by someone with wolfsbane and she—" I tried to keep my composure. "I wasn't thinking. I left her alone and then ran head-first into danger. Naphinae took the hit for me." I could feel all of my strength slipping. Watching her like this was too much but I couldn't leave her.

The doctor tore Naphinae's shirt open at her shoulder and started working on removing the arrow. Her veins were turning purple, the wolfsbane was spreading, fast. Naphinae didn't flinch. She was completely unconscious, she had surrendered to her pain. The doctor was moving quickly and Shade jumped in offering her help where she could. I wanted nothing more than to take her pain away.

"I can help." I blurted out as I wiped away a stray tear.

The doctor turned to me and gestured for me to come over and take her hand. "The easy part is over, what happens next is most likely going to snap her back to reality."

I came over and gently took her hand in mine as Shade did the same on the other side of Naphinae. "Okay… I can do this." She was cold to the touch. I could feel her slipping away from the bond we shared. I couldn't lose her… Not like this. The doctor pulled out a metal rod and a lighter, placing it to the side. The doctor put on gloves and a syringe slowly starting to pull the poison from her wound. The purple in her veins slowly receding.

"Please stay with me, little one." I held her hand tighter, kissing the top of her hand and stroking the hair from her face. Her hair was still wet from her shower, frozen in certain parts from the cold of the blizzard.

The doctor threw the syringe in a waste bin and turned back to me and Shade. "Ready for the worst of it?" Shade and I exchanged looks and nodded at the doctor to continue.

The doctor picked up the metal rod and the lighter. She heated the rod until about an inch of one end turned red before sticking it into Naphinae's wound.

Naphinae reacted almost immediately, shutting her eyes tighter and screaming out in agony as the heated metal cauterized her wound. "Little one, you can do this… I'm right here with you." I brushed the hair from her face and kissed her forehead, holding her hand tighter as she squeezed.

"We got you Naph, it's okay." Shade chimed in.

The doctor pushed the heated metal further into her wound, small purple vapors releasing as the flesh burned. The pain was unbearable, Naphinae couldn't bear it anymore. She let out a pained scream, writhing in agony as she screamed out in pain. "Don't give up… we're almost there." I hated seeing her like this, but she had to be strong to fight this.

When the doctor finished cauterizing the wound, Naphinae let out a breath and relaxed. "I'll patch up the wound to prevent an infection but she'll need to stay in bed for a few days. She won't have much strength and she'll probably try to refuse food but she needs to eat."

I looked down at Naphinae and felt myself relax knowing she would be okay. "Thank you, doctor. I'll make sure she stays in bed and eats."

It took a few hours for the wound to be fully closed and healed. I carried Naphinae back to our room and Shade helped me change her clothes so she'd be comfortable.

When I woke up, I was in different clothes and my shoulder hurt like hell.

The events of what happened came flooding back to me as I sat up holding my shoulder. I was alone in the room as usual and got up from the bed, walking into the bathroom. I was a wreck, I brushed my hair and teeth.

I heard shuffling coming from the room over. "Little one? Are you alright?" He walked into the room.

"What the hell happened last night?" I walked out of the bathroom and back into the bedroom.

"You were attacked by someone with wolfsbane… but I was able to get you help in time."

I nodded. "No, I remember that. I mean when we got back, that's where I go blank." I walked back to the bed and sat down rubbing my shoulder.

He walked over and sat down next to me on the bed. "It's normal to lose time in these situations... the important thing is that you made it," he said gently, trying to comfort me. "You were lucky that we got you help in time... otherwise, things could have ended very badly."

I looked down. "I'm sorry for putting you through all of this. I should have been more careful."

He wrapped his arm around me and was careful not to hit my wound. "Little One... don't be sorry. You didn't do anything wrong. You were attacked... it's not your fault," he said gently, trying to reassure me. "I just want you to be okay and I will do whatever it takes to make sure that you are."

I kept my head down suddenly remembering the argument we had before the attack. "Little one, are you alright?" I nodded and pulled away from him, crawling back into bed and getting under the blanket.

"Yeah, just tired." I didn't look at him, I just closed my eyes wanting to ignore how I was really feeling.

"Please talk to me… I know you're hurting, but you don't have to face it alone. You can lean on me for support." I tightened the blanket around me wanting to hide from the pain in my heart, it would never be me. He can care all he wants but it won't ever be me. "Little one, don't hide from your emotions. You have every right to feel hurt and sad… you have every right to express those feelings."

I sat up and looked at him, letting the blanket fall back down against the bed. "You really want me to express how I feel?"

"Yes," he said simply.

I got up from the bed and stood right in front of him, looking up at him. "I can't stand this! You mark me as your mate but it is always about the pack! I can't even have you for a fucking weekend!"

He looked down at me, not breaking eye contact. "Little One... I know that I have been focusing on the pack lately... but you are my mate. I promise that once this situation with the rogues is sorted out, we will have all the time in the world for ourselves. I know that it's been difficult lately... but please believe me when I say that I want to be with you."

I was shocked. "I'm sorry? Rogues?"

He seemed remorseful. "I should have told you sooner... but there have been reports of rogue werewolves in the area," he said gently, trying to reassure me. "These werewolves have been attacking people and causing trouble. We've been trying to track them down but they've been hard to find."

I stepped back from him. I couldn't believe what I was hearing. "Why is this the first I hear about it?" I suddenly felt even more angry than before.

"Please don't be angry. I wanted to protect you. I should've told you sooner but I didn't want to worry." He stepped closer to me and I put my hands up taking another step back.

"No, no. You do not get to do that every time! If you want me to be your luna, your mate… Then you need to treat me as an equal." I put on my shoes and started walking toward the door. "Fix this or I walk, 'cause you don't treat me as a luna let alone a mate." I walked out of the room and walked down the hallway of the pack house to get outside, I needed air.

I walked around the borders of our territory for a while until I reached the clearing, the pups were having a snowball fight. I tried to walk past them but they all started giggling and pelting me with snowballs. I did my best to enjoy spending time with the pups but it was hard with an injured shoulder. No matter what I did, my mind kept wandering back to my fight with Greyson. I wanted him here to enjoy playing with the pups with me.

Eventually, all the pups left the clearing and I decided it was time for me to head back too. I was covered in snow from head to toe, I was cold and sore but it was worth it to see all the youngest pack members smiling.

I walked back into our bedroom and saw him sitting in his office as I passed by. I kicked off my shoes and went to go take a much needed shower. Greyson walked into our room. "Little one, you're back. I was starting to worry about you." I walked up to the mirror in the bathroom and started to remove the gauze from my shoulder so I could take a proper shower.

"Yup," was all I said in response.

There was a brief awkward silence. "How is your shoulder doing?"

I walked over to the shower and turned on the water. "Sore, but fine. I'll live." I started taking off my clothes.

He walked into the bathroom and stopped at the doorway. "Do you need any help?"

I finished taking off my clothes and put them in the laundry bag. "Nope." I started walking back toward the shower.

"Are you sure? You look like you could use some help…"

I stopped in my tracks and spun on my heels, looking at him. "I am not a helpless pup." I raised an eyebrow. "If I need help I am perfectly capable of asking." I turned back toward the shower and stepped in, letting the water run down my body.

"I just want to make sure that you're okay. If you need anything or if you change your mind… please let me know." I heard him leave the bedroom closing the door behind himself.

Chapter Twenty-Four

The second I heard the door close I broke down in tears leaning against the cold tiled wall of the shower. I wanted to beg, I wanted to scream and be what he needed, but I have been. This isn't on me, this isn't my fault.

I stood in the shower for a while, I couldn't tell if it was helping me feel better or not. I got out of the shower and dried off after turning off the water. Going into the closet I couldn't decide between comfort or something more professional. Clearly, this issue with the rogues isn't being handled well. I went for comfort, putting on one of Greyson's hoodies and a pair of knitted tights. I slipped my shoes back on and walked into the office.

Greyson was sitting at his desk with Tristan, Ashley, and Cody sitting opposite him. "Little one… I didn't expect to see you here. Is everything alright?" As Greyson was speaking to me I could see Ashely's smirk a mile away.

"Oh, sorry… Am I intruding?" My tone was more sarcastic than I had intended.

"No, you're not intruding. We were just discussing the rogue attacks. Are you okay?" I knew he was trying to be cautious with me but Ashely's presence alone was driving me insane. If she wasn't pregnant I would've wiped that smug smirk off her face.

"I'm perfectly fine. Any discussions about the pack's safety concerns me as well… I mean after all." I walked up behind Ashley and leaned down for her to hear me clearly. "I am the pack's luna." Although I could see a hint of pride in Greyson's expression he wasn't happy with how I was reacting to Ashley.

"Naphinae, I know that you're worried about the pack's safety, but you need to remember your place. You are luna… yes, but I am the alpha. I have the final say on everything that happens in this pack."

I stood up and looked at him. All I could see was red. "Tristan, please escort yourself as well as Cody and Ashley out of this office. I think I need to have a word with the alpha."

I could see Greyson's demeanor shifted. "Naphinae… I don't think—"

Before he could finish his sentence Tristan spoke up. "Of course luna. We will leave it to you." Tristan gestured for Ashley and Cody to follow him out of the office. It was obvious Tristan knew something Greyson didn't.

It was just me and Greyson left in the office. I turned to Greyson, my fists clenched, my eyes brimming with tears, but I didn't feel as sad as I usually had been. This, this was anger.

"Little one, please don't cry. You need to remember your place in this pack... I am the alpha and you are my luna. That doesn't mean I don't care about you, but you can't challenge me like that."

I scoffed. "You have got to be kidding me. This dominance thing may work on everyone else, but you can leave that in the bedroom as far as I'm concerned." I placed my hands on the desk and leaned forward looking him dead in the eye. "Isn't the role of luna the alpha female? And if so doesn't that mean I have just as much authority? Yes, you get the final say. But you kept this from me. I know my place, do you?"

His eyes watched my every move. "Naphinae... do not try to teach me how things work in this pack. I have been alpha for many years and I know what is best for us. Just because you are luna does not mean that you can do whatever you want," he said sharply, his tone leaving no room for negotiation.

My eyes flashed with anger, and I let out a growl. "It's time for me to teach you a lesson." I felt the urge to show him how wrong he was.

"You can't fight me… it's against pack law."

I stood up and started walking toward the door to the office. "I'm not fighting anymore." I shrugged. What I was about to do was going to hurt, but I couldn't do this anymore. "If this is the way you want things to go… Then your wish is my command… Alpha." I walked out of his office, sending Tristan, Cody, and Ashley back in to continue their meeting.

I left the pack house entirely looking for Shade and Ryker. I walked around until I found both Ryker and Shade, they were training. I watched for a moment, Shade was pulling her punches but so was Ryker. They obviously care for one another and they were blinded by the fear of them being rejected.

I didn't want to interrupt but I didn't see another choice. "Ryker, Shade." I approached them as they pulled away from one another like a couple of teenagers who just got caught doing something they shouldn't.

"Luna." Ryker nodded.

"Naph!" Shade ran up to me and hugged me tightly.

I groaned in response. "A little too tight Shade." I patted her back. She stepped back and bowed her head, "I need your help, both of you." My eyes darted between the two of them and they nodded, listening intently.

We walked for a while to be out of earshot of the rest of the lingering pack. We stopped by the lake. I told them of what happened at Greyson's family cabin. "The hunters may not be our biggest concern now, but if we don't solve this rogue issue then the hunters might end up being our biggest concern." Shade seemed afraid but Ryker, he seemed deep in thought. "Ryker? What is it?"

He was pulled from his thought for a moment. "It may be beneficial for you to pay Gunner a visit."

Shade looked at him and shook her head. "No, you can't send her to him."

Ryker remained looking at me. "He was a rogue but he proved his worth to the pack and Greyson welcomed him back." Ryker didn't seem sure but he couldn't see another option.

"Where does he live?" I was worried but showed no fear.

"Naph, you can't be serious. Gunner is dangerous." Shade's concern was more and more evident by the second. "The outskirts of the pack's territory." Shade lowered her head as she spoke, she knew I wasn't backing down.

"Be careful luna. Gunner won't hesitate to hurt you if he sees you as a threat."

I thanked both Ryker and Shade and left to go find Gunner.

Chapter Twenty-Five

The sun was starting to set by the time I'd found Gunner's home. His home was secluded on the very edge of the pack territory. I started approaching the front door when someone called out, "Ah, you must be the new Luna. You smell just like Greyson but with a sweeter tinge in your scent."

I stiffened hearing the masculine tone but turned in the direction of where it came from. A man crouched down tending to a small garden, his clothes weren't expensive looking but not rags either. "I take it you must be Gunner."

The man stood to his feet, wiping his hands on a rag he kept tucked in his back pocket, he extended a hand toward me. "Gunner Greene."

I took his hand and shook it firmly. "Naphinae Kent. I apologize for both my appearance and for disturbing your solitude."

He chuckled and shook his head as he pulled his hand away. "No need to be apologetic luna. How can I help you?"

I smiled. "Straight to it then?" He nodded and bowed his head as a sign of respect.

I did my best to explain the situation and the dangers I have faced. "So, you want to more about rogues?" I nodded. "There isn't much to tell unfortunately luna."

I cut him off. "Please, luna is my title but not who I am. Call me Naph."

He chuckled and smiled at me. "Okay then, Naph. Rogues… They are either banished or have left their packs willingly. You can sniff them out easily if you know what you're looking for. If rogues have rallied and are causing problems then no one is safe, they don't abide by any pack laws." He seemed calm but I could feel his concern radiating from him.

"Is there any way to neutralize the threat they pose?"

He looked at me stunned. "Naph, it won't be easy. They kill because they want to, they won't hesitate if you threaten them."

"I understand. I appreciate your advice, but whatever happens is for the safety of the pack." I smiled at him attempting to reassure him.

We spoke briefly about what was happening with the pack. "You've mentioned everyone but Greyson. Don't tell me that the alpha and luna are fighting."

I lowered my head. "I'd prefer not to talk about that. Personal reasons."

He nodded and placed his hand on my shoulder. "I get it. I became a rogue because my mate had rejected me, it started with emotion and then rejecting the bond altogether. It took everything that made me who I was. I became a shell of my former self." I looked back up at him. "If you need a space to call your own… There's an abandoned home by the creek. It needs work but seeing the determination in those beautiful hazel eyes of yours, I'm sure you'll do just fine."

My eyes searched his. Was he hitting on me? I shook it off and smiled. "Thank you Gunner, I'll put a good word in with the alpha for you."

He shook his head. "No need." He pulled me into a tight hug.

We said our goodbyes and I went out to search for the home he had spoken of. I found it after an hour of walking. It was run down for sure, but the more walked around and looked at the repairs needed… I could definitely make this work.

I went back to Gunner's house and borrowed some tools and started working on the house the second I got back to it. Gunner told me to keep his tools as long as I needed them. There were trees surrounding the house and it was mostly wooden, it was more a cabin with flare. I spent hours working on fixing the house. Time completely escaped me and my shoulder was more sore than it was yesterday.

The sun was just coming up so I packed up Gunner's tool and made my way back to the pack house for some food and possibly a nap.

When I walked into the kitchen, Rowan and Cody greeted me kindly and offered to make me food since I missed pack breakfast. I politely declined and made something small since I was oddly nauseous. I made a quick sandwich and cleaned up after myself and ate as I walked back to the bedroom Greyson and I were sharing. When I walked into the room Greyson was sleeping so I did my best to stay quiet and go take a shower. I wanted to get back to fixing up that house as quickly as I could.

"Little one… What happened? Why didn't you come home last night?" I could hear how tired he was.

"I needed time," I said simply as I walked into the bathroom. I started taking my clothes off, but once I took off my shirt I saw how bad my shoulder looked.

He walked into the bathroom but was pried from his exhaustion when he saw my shoulder. "What happened to your shoulder?" He walked up to me and examined the wound. "Did you hurt it again?"

"No, I didn't. Does it look bad?" I looked over at him.

"I think you should go see the pack medic. You could have torn something." He rubbed his hand over my shoulder and I winced, I didn't realize how much it hurt until now.

"I'll go, just let me take a shower first."

"Yes, of course." He let my shoulder go and I finished getting undressed and started the water. "Just let me know if you need anything. I'll be right here."

I showered as quickly as I could and got dressed. Greyson was waiting for me, sitting on the edge of the bed. "Okay. Ready."

"Let's go." He stood up offering me his hand.

We got to the medic's office and she seemed concerned as she examined my shoulder. Greyson stood by my side, holding my hand tightly, offering me his support. "How bad is it? Is it something serious?" Greyson cut the silence.

The medic shook her head. "Nothing serious, it seems agitated at best. Luna, have you been doing anything strenuous?"

I shook my head. "A few repairs to some stuff but no, I felt fine."

Greyson didn't seem impressed by my answer. "Just repairs to some stuff, huh?" His eyes narrowed at me. "Are you sure you haven't been doing anything else?"

I snapped my head in his direction. "What are you implying?"

He shook his head. "I don't want to assume anything, but I know you haven't been telling me everything."

I crossed my arms, looking away from him. "I don't want to talk about it."

"You know I can't just let this go." I refused to look at him.

"Maybe you should step out, alpha, I can take care of her." The medic chimed in.

"I'm sorry, what did you just say?" He sounded even angrier.

The medic stepped in between us, putting her hand on my injured shoulder. "Let me take over, I'll handle it."

"Excuse me?" he said softly, trying to stay calm. "I'm the alpha of this pack and it's my responsibility to take care of my luna. I don't need your help." He added firmly, not wanting the medic to interfere.

"Then why bring her here? You aren't allowing me to do my job." The medic insisted. Her hands were cold which made my shoulder feel a bit better, but the pressure she was applying was making me whimper.

He didn't like being questioned like this, especially when it came to the care of me. "I brought her here because you are a pack medic. It is your job to help me take care of my luna," he said firmly, trying to get the medic to understand his point of view. "I am not allowing you to do anything other than provide medical attention for my luna." He added softly, trying not to sound too harsh.

"Then let me do my job and step outside." The medic huffed, trying to keep her composure. "You wouldn't have brought her to me if you could help her, and arguing isn't helping." She looked at him over her shoulder, but her hands remained on my wound.

"Fine." Greyson left the room. "Just be careful with her…" he shouted through the door.

"Luna, be honest with me. What did you do yesterday?" Her voice was hushed and calm.

"I was doing repairs, I'm being honest. I didn't shift, I didn't do anything that would've agitated my shoulder."

She nodded and kept applying pressure on my shoulder. "Okay, here's what we're going to do." She let go of my shoulder and stepped away for a moment before coming back with a needle.

"Umm… what is that?"

She chuckled at my obvious fear. "It's an antibiotic for any possible infection. This'll be quick I promise." She stabbed the needle into my shoulder and I almost felt better instantly. "You may just have a small amount of the wolfsbane you were shot with still in your system. Come back and see me in a week or two when you have the time and I'll take another look." She smiled at me and threw out the needle in her waste bin.

"Can I ask something?" She nodded and walked back over so I wouldn't strain myself to see her. "Wolfsbane, how does it work? Like is there a way we could immunize ourselves to it?"

She thought on my question for a moment before responding, "In theory, but it's very risky. Why do you ask?"

I looked down at my hands. "I've been thinking about it since I got shot with the arrow. I think it's smart to try but the risks outweigh the possibility of trying."

She nodded and sighed. "I understand luna. But unfortunately, it isn't something we can do without the risk of losing a pack member to experimenting with something like that."

I looked back up at her with a smile. "Thank you for your help, and I'm sorry about his behavior."

She smiled. "The next time you go to rebuild that abandoned house. Take someone with you to help. Yes, I know and no, I won't tell alpha." I was stunned as to how she knew but didn't push, I simply nodded and left.

Greyson approached me the second I walked out of the office. "Little one… How are you feeling?"

I raised an eyebrow at him, I was still furious with him. "I'm fine. She said it could be a small portion of wolfsbane still in my system, she gave me a shot of antibiotics for it. I need to come back in a couple of weeks to check in."

He let out a breath and his expression softened. "Can we talk?" He broke eye contact with me, seeming nervous. "I know you're still angry with me… but we need to sort things out between us."

In a huff, I turned and started to walk away from Greyson.

"Stop!" He was growing more frustrated and I could feel it. "We need to talk about what happened yesterday." His voice was firm and commanding.

I scoffed and turned to face him. "Is that an order alpha?" I only ever called him by his title when he was like this, and if he continued this way he'd lose me.

He took a deep breath, trying to stay calm. "No… it's not an order."

I smirked and raised an eyebrow as I turned away from him, starting to walk off again. "Good, because I wouldn't have listened anyway."

He took a deep breath and took a few steps, following behind me. He grabbed my arm. "Stop. We need to talk about what happened yesterday."

I turned to face him. "Alright… let's talk."

"Thank you, little one." He let go of my arm and took a step back. "What happened last night… Why did you storm out on me?" His tone was soft but I was still pissed.

"Am I just supposed to defend myself with everyone but you? Don't let Alexander belittle me, but you can?" I crossed my arms over my chest. "I don't know what you expected, Greyson. You say you care about me then treat me lesser than. I matter to you, I'm so important to you, I'm everything to you… Until I'm not and I stand up to you."

He seemed frustrated but held it back and remaining calm. "I don't want to belittle you, and I certainly don't want to treat you lesser than anyone else in the pack," he said softly, trying to keep his voice calm and steady. "You are important to me… more important than anyone else in this world. But as the alpha, I can't always show favoritism towards you."

I scoffed and looked away. "You never do… It's always the pack, and when I show concern for the pack the way any proper luna would… You treat me as an omega not your luna." I could feel my tears threatening to fall.

"Please don't cry. I know that I haven't always shown you the love and appreciation that you deserve, but I want you to know that I do care about you. You are my luna… My everything."

I turned facing him, my tears remaining unshed but welling up further. "I'm calling your bluff, you talk a good game but your words don't match your actions."

"Little one… what do you want from me? How can I prove to you that I care about you? That my words match my actions?"

I closed my eyes, my tears finally falling. "You asked me closer to when we first met what my idea of a perfect mate is… I don't need you to be perfect…" I took a breath trying to keep my voice steady. "I need you to stop being my alpha and be my mate. Love me enough that every now and then you'll pick me, spending time with me. Love me enough to trust the hierarchy we've put in place so we can have time away together."

I opened my eyes and he was stunned. "Little one…" He reached out and softly wiped away my tears. "You are right… I haven't been the mate that you deserve. But I do love you… more than anything else in this world. From now on, I will be your mate first and foremost. I will make sure to spend more time with you… make you feel loved."

I looked up at him, my eyes still wet with tears but a hint of hope in them. "You will?" I whispered, wiping away my tears with the back of my hand.

"Yes, Little One… I promise," he said softly, caressing my cheek and brushing away a tear with his thumb. "From now on, you are my mate first. We are equals… and I will make sure to give you the time and attention that you deserve as my luna and my mate." I leaned into his touch, feeling comforted. I wanted to believe him but he had hurt me so much already.

"How do I know I can trust what you're saying?"

He caressed my cheek with his thumb, "There's nothing I can say right now that would make you immediately trust me again." He took a step back and looked me in the eyes. "But I am here for you… and I will do anything and everything in my power to show you how much I love you and care about you."

I looked away, still feeling hurt and unsure. "Trust me, I want to believe you. I really do, but I need time to heal." I teared up again, feeling hurt by the memories of our past.

"Little one… take all the time you need. I know it will take time for you to trust me again, and I am willing to do anything and everything to prove myself worthy of your love," he said softly, reaching out to caress my cheek again. "I love you… and I will do whatever it takes to regain your trust."

I pulled away. "I need to go." I turned away and started to walk out of the pack house again.

"Please don't go" He took a step forward, placing his hand on my shoulder. "Stay with me… let's talk about this together."

I turned and offered him a weak smile. "I feel like it's too much too fast. You asked me about what my idea of a perfect mate is earlier in our relationship and now you're acting like I never asked." I looked down, I didn't want to be here or talking about this anymore.

"I did… I know, I know." He stepped forward cupping my face in his hands. "I am doing my best to live up to those expectations, I want to be the mate you deserve… Please… stay with me and let's work through this together."

I pulled away again. "Please… I need some space. I can't, won't, keep doing this with you. I have to go." I walked out of the pack house not letting him stop me this time, without looking back.

He followed after me. "Little one… Please!" He called after me. "Don't leave me… I can't do this without you." He stepped in my path, blocking me from leaving.

I didn't look at him. "You have been doing it without me, this entire time…" I turned away from him, holding myself. "Luna is just a title… You don't allow me the space to help the pack grow saying it's your way of protecting me… You say I'm your mate but time and time again you prove that means nothing to you." I wiped away a stray tear, refusing to turn around and look at him. "I can't keep putting you before me. I won't, not anymore." A brief silence took over.

"I understand that you're upset with me. And I know that I have hurt you in the past." He took a step forward and gently turned me around to face him.

"It's not just the past." My tears started falling. "I can't take the uncertainty anymore. I can't be the mate you want me to be when you won't let me be who I am." I continued, trying to keep my voice steady.

"Little one… you are my mate. But I know that I have not always treated you like the amazing woman that you are." He took a step forward and gently wiped away my tears. "I want to make it up to you… I want to prove myself worthy of your love."

I shook my head and moved his hands away from my face. "I'm sorry… I can't." My voice was barely audible. "Please, respect my wishes."

Without another word, I ran off leaving Greyson standing alone in front of the pack house. I could feel his heartbreak through our bond as I ran. It killed me but I had to keep going.

Chapter Twenty-Six

I ran back to the house I had started repairing and threw myself into fixing it. I spent days patching holes and going over the landscaping. I did my best to keep myself on track, but I found myself thinking about Greyson constantly.

A part of me felt like shifting and running free but I couldn't. Thinking of shifting reminded me of my first shift and how Greyson helped me through it. I spent days with little rest and little food as I worked tirelessly to finish fixing the house. When I slept, I slept on the ground. My shoulder started to feel better but the soreness I felt only persisted. Even when I wasn't thinking of Greyson, I could feel him, his pain.

I had to go back to the pack house to meet with the medic for a check-in about my shoulder. I prayed that I wouldn't run into Greyson and thankfully I didn't.

I got to her office and she greeted me kindly. "Good morning my luna." She bowed her head as a sign of respect.

"Good morning." I smiled and bowed my head in return, my smile wasn't genuine, I had nothing to be happy about.

"How's your shoulder?" She got straight to the point and gestured for me to take a seat while she closed the door.

I sat on the bed and pulled my shirt off and one of my bra straps down. "Sore, but nothing I can't handle."

She came over and looked at my shoulder closer after she put on a pair of gloves. "Luna, is it alright if I take some of your blood?"

I looked at her confused. "I'm sorry?"

She chuckled. "Forgive me, I should've elaborated. I want to check for any residual traces of wolfsbane in your system. You're healing nicely but I just want to be sure."

I let out a breath and nodded. "Okay, yeah, no that makes sense." She gathered everything she needed and got started.

It hurt at first obviously but she made it quick and kept me distracted by carrying on a simple conversation with me. After she finished she sent me on my way and I left the pack house without running into Greyson. I went back to my house and couldn't bring myself to do anything.

Days passed, days full of nothing. There was a knock on my door but I wasn't expecting anyone. I opened it and Gunner stood outside admiring the work I had done.

"Good morning Gunner, how can I help you? Did you need your tools back?" I felt a bit worried but he just laughed and shook his head.

"No, Luna. I came to check on you."

I furrowed my eyebrows. "Oh." Neither of us said anything for a few moments. "Actually, I had a question." Gunner raised an eyebrow waiting for me to continue. "Rejection… Does it hurt?" I lowered my head feeling ashamed for even considering rejection as an option, I'm just so tired of fighting for Greyson's love, I don't see any other way out.

Gunner sighed and took a few minutes before answering me. "If I'm honest, yes… Rejection… it's capable of killing your wolf if you aren't strong enough to handle it. Rejection isn't always the answer, it won't happen if both mates involved don't accept the rejection. Why do you ask luna?"

I kept my head down as I answered. "I… I'm not sure if Greyson and I work as mates." Saying that out loud stung more than I cared to admit.

"Naph…" I looked up at Gunner, his jade-green eyes reflecting my pain. "Are you sure that's what you want?" I took a deep breath and sighed. "Naph, being a mate is more than thinking of yourself."

"I know that! All I've done is think of him!" I shouted and he didn't say anything, he hugged me.

"I'm sorry. I didn't mean to make you angry. It isn't my place to question you." I wasn't expecting him to react this way.

I pulled away from Gunner and took a step back. "No, It's fine." I was confused by his kindness. Gunner doesn't seem like the monster Ryker or Shade made him seem.

"Naph, you need to think on this thoroughly. Once it's done, there's no going back."

I nodded. "I understand." Before the conversation could continue, I felt a sharp pain on my ride side ribcage that sent me to the floor screaming out in pain. I was fine, I wasn't bleeding, I hadn't been attacked.

"Naph!" Gunner immediately knelt next to me, his hand now on my back. "What's wrong?! What are you feeling?!" He seemed panicked but I couldn't speak, the pain completely left me breathless. This wasn't my pain.

"Greyson…" I screamed out again, falling flat against the floor. My back suddenly felt like it had been torn open. I could feel every tear, every claw mark as if it were my own.

"Stay here, I'll go find him." Gunner got to his feet in a hurry, closing the door. I heard him shift and take off, I didn't have the strength to follow suit and help.

I felt powerless. Greyson was facing a relentless attack. I could feel every scratch and bite every thud from him falling. Whatever fight he was facing, I could only hope that Gunner could get to him in time. His strength was wavering and I could feel him slipping from our bond. He wasn't going to make it. I lay on the floor in pure agony, crying from the pain that wasn't my own.

I did my best, but unsure if it would work, I focused on the bond and lent Greyson every ounce of strength I could. 'Lean on me, use me. I'm here' I hoped my thoughts could reach him. With how we've been and our bond not being strong I wasn't sure if anything would work. All I could do was sit here, useless and in pain.

The pain started to subside and there were no signs of Gunner. I didn't know what was happening, I didn't know if anyone was safe. I didn't have enough strength or energy to shift. I had no choice but to walk back to the pack house.

It took hours to get back, I've never felt so drained. "Naphinae!" Shade shouted, she ran up to me and caught me before my legs gave out.

"Where—Where is he?" I struggled to get the words out. I could hardly breathe, my anxiety was setting in and my heart was breaking at every possible thought.

"He's okay… He's with the medics… Do— Do you want me to take you?" She held me tight so I wouldn't fall over. I nodded completely overtaken by everything I was feeling.

Shade led me to the medics office and away from the pack members huddled up outside the pack house. The sight in front of me, in that office, was something I wouldn't wish on my enemies.

Greyson, Tristan, Gunner… All three of them were laid out, bleeding. I made no sound but my tears fell like a waterfall driven by the rapids.

"No…" I shook my head and couldn't tear my eyes away from what I was looking at. Shade tried to bring me outside but my feet wouldn't move, I couldn't. He needed me and I was so blinded by my feelings that I wasn't there when he needed me. Suddenly it hit me.

"Where's Ashley?" Her pup, she's pregnant. If I could feel Greyson's pain… I couldn't imagine what she was feeling. And Gunner, he had no one… The pack… With Greyson injured this badly, I had to step up… I had to be the luna they needed right now.

I stood to my feet, trembling. I left the medic's office and hurried to Greyson's office. I needed to know what happened, a clue, something, anything. This had to be the rogues, maybe hunters, possibly both.

I slammed his office door open and ran up to his desk. I sifted through all the papers on his desk and started organizing them.

Nothing, there was nothing on why this would've happened. I sat in his chair, defeated. How can I hope to help without any information? I took a minute to collect myself.

Something in my bond to Greyson shifted and my heart sank… He was dying.

I got up from his chair and bolted back to the medic's office. The medic was standing over him trying everything to get him back. He didn't have a pulse, he was going pale.

I ran up to the bed he was on and took his hand in mine without hesitation. "Luna, you can't touch him right now." She had defibrillators in her hands.

"I don't care, do it. I'm not letting him go." I held his hand tighter taking his other hand too. She hesitated.

"Luna—" She attempted to tell me again.

"DO IT!" I snapped, now crying. She nodded and started to shock him again. I felt every surge of the electric shock, he wasn't responding to it. "Greyson Carver, you stubborn son of a bitch. This is not how our story ends. This is not how you die." I didn't know what else to do. My pain was palpable. I snapped my head toward her. "Keep going." She seemed like she was about to say he was gone. "AGAIN, THAT'S AN ORDER DAMNIT!" She shocked him again and I held his hands tighter, nothing. "Turn it all the way up."

She seemed worried but she did. "Luna, you need to let go." I shook my head. "Luna—"

"NO!" I was set in my choices. I wasn't ever leaving him, no rejection, no more fighting, I wasn't leaving things like this.

"LUNA!" she shouted.

I raised an eyebrow as I looked up at her, tearing my gaze from Greyson's lifeless body. "I can't let you do this, I've turned up the defibrillators up all the way but I can't do this with you still holding him." She looked at me with extreme concern.

"And why the fuck not?" I challenged her defiance.

Her gaze fell from my eyes to my stomach then back up to my eyes. She didn't need to say anything else, I understood completely.

I reluctantly let him go and took a step back. She shocked him at least five times at full power before his pulse came back. We both let out a breath and I came back to his side in a hurry, stroking his hair and holding his hand tightly.

"Grey…" I whispered. "Come back to me… Take your time, but come back to me…" I continued stroking his hair and held his hand in mine over my stomach.

I had no idea how or when, but… Our first pup… I was pregnant.